THE CREATIVE WRITERS

*A BURLESQUE OF THE IMAGINATION
ON TOTALITARIAN THEMES
IN THE MANNER OF ÉMILE COHL
& LES ARTS INCOHÉRENTS,
HARRY EVERETT SMITH &
HANNA-BARBERA*

GARY AMDAHL

GALLEON

Actual Praise For Gary Amdahl

"Yo G, I'm editing a book now with the hope I can scoot off to Norway by the end of June. Please use that old quote.* As I gaze at my looming 85th birthday, I pray I'll never read another novel. Excuse the brevity but I've mislaid my eyedrops."

* "Gary Amdahl's vivid stories are at once lyrical and unexpectedly in your face. American wrath here puts on its several seductive faces and native charm, suggesting our worst side has grown as comfortable as an old shoe. A book [*Visigoth*] we'll remember."
　—Thomas McGuane

"Amdahl is one whose gifts are staggering and hard won. The stories [in *I Am Death* and *The Intimidator Still Lives In Our Hearts*] relate, by the way of guts through grace, the wholeness of a novel too good for mere philosophy. Gary Amdahl knows sports, men, women, and dogs, thank God, so thoroughly as to make them myth. Camus comes to mind, thought with great muscle."
　—Barry Hannah

Amdahl's unnamed narrator [in *Across My Big Brass Bed*] is a reimagined Orpheus, a rebel, a musician, an addict, and a sex god, and his tales of motorcycles, Bach, heroin, abortions, Martin Buber, and the bandoneón will astound you."
　—Paul Charles Griffin in *Rain Taxi*

"Speed and dexterity race against implausibly careful dream recollections, whose luxuriously slowed detail is Amdahl's forte, here with the manic affect of a dying man pleading to live, the clock running out, yet him unwilling to miss explaining a single moment. Telling the stories, including one lovely long section almost entirely a mystical-hallucinatory mash-up of busy self-testing in the dream ecology of a lake, and in it, diving but not dying. It may keep him alive for at least the long night and day it has taken to write the 'involuntary memory' so far, Henry James on a dirt bike, a Don Juan of self-loathing, liberated lothario who can't help perform the conquest but wishes it were more egalitarian."
—Andrew Tonkovich in the *Los Angeles Review of Books*

"Why does the title 'Franz Kafka, PhD, Professor of Creative Writing, Charles University, Prague' raise a smile to our lips?"
—J. M. Coetzee, "Eight Ways of Looking at Samuel Beckett"

"Clichés, stock phrases, adherence to conventional, standardized codes of expression and conduct have the socially recognized function of protecting us against reality."
—Hannah Arendt, *The Life of the Mind*

"The static, the finite, and the solid had seen their day."
—Henri Michaux, *Major Ordeals of the Mind and Countless Minor Ones*

The Creative Writers: A Burlesque of the Imagination on Totalitarian Themes in the Manner of Émile Cohl & Les Arts Incohérents, Harry Everett Smith & Hanna-Barbera

© Gary Amdahl 2024
All rights reserved.

First Galleon Edition, September 2024
ISBN 978-1-998122-127

Published by Galleon Books
Moncton, New Brunswick, Canada
www.galleonbooks.ca

Cover image is James Ensor's *Squelette Arrêtant Masques* (1891)

This is a work of fiction. What about "fiction" don't you understand? We don't mean to sound testy; it's a sincere question. Our feeling is that it is what it is, even if no one knows what it is that it is. Though of course we know what we like: "You call that art?" A work of memory and imagination? Yes, perforce. We are made by our times and places, but artists transcend that making as they wander through the fog and silence of the oldest urge in human consciousness: "What is going on in my head? Must I tell the others?" Which is a long way around this boilerplate: any and all resemblances to actual people living or dead, e.g., Jackie Gleason, Sojourner Truth, and the rest of my cast of characters, is not only unintentional but all in YOUR head.

Library and Archives Canada Cataloguing in Publication is available upon request.

for Leslie, all ways, always

and in memory of Dwight Yates
who read everything I wrote
and who was a particular champion of this novel

1

In which our principal argument is introduced, that the Creative Writers are foolish pawns in a cruel game of totalitarian subjugatory Amusement unto Death. George Swan, an adjunct professor of Creative Effort is introduced and physically translated.

Two figures pass unseen down the hallway. The first is a woman in a skin-tight, diamond-white suit and balaclava with the black half of the *taijitu* on her chest. The second is a man in a skin-tight suit and balaclava so black it appears to be a body-shaped hole in space, with the white half of the *taijitu* on his chest.

Alice Reznya, the Dunning-Kruger Chair for Creative Effort, and Orgí Paráfora, the Francis Galton Chair for Epigenetics in Literature, are chatting in the hallway, thinking maybe they should finish the conversation in one or the other's office.

"Have you," asks Orgí with her signature nervous hostility, "signed the Non-Disclosure Agreement?"

"No," says Alice with her signature brisk superiority. "What's it about?"

"I don't know."

"Who's signed it?"

"Everybody. We have to."

"But then we ought to know what it's about, no?"

"No, no, no. Listen to me. It's about agreeing to not disclose, i.e., 'know,' in effect, what it's about."

Maintaining her brisk superiority, Alice confirms the necessity of protection from legal exposure. "It's probably something to do with non-disparagement."

Gary Amdahl

...

The Dean, Ken Brown, a white boy with dreads, aka Kenny B or Kenny B Dean, has just sent around a memo outlining his signature project, a new major in Spiritual Entrepreneurship. "And let me remind you all that the deadline for the Five Adjectives is nearly upon us," he post-scripts. "Which five words do you think best express academic life here at our house?" This is controversial because the creative writers feel that only they are qualified to develop such a list. Orgí has a quick face-to-face with the dean and secures a course-release that means she will never have to teach again, and another student assistant to research adjectives, before the rest of the creative writers know what's hit them. She says they will have a long-list of a thousand words by the end of the month. Orgí had long ago turned the dean's head, with her "clear attunement to the tenor of the times" and her thoughtful gift-giving: fruit baskets to the creative writers, students and colleagues alike, and whoever else around campus has done her a favor or paid her a compliment, featuring "pear cider made from 100% pear," unaware of the quote's origin in a Stewart Lee bit—Stewart Lee being the forty-first best comedian in the world. At the door, she chuckles and says that she has read recently some radical thinkers on the decreasing adequacy of language to describe things like—she quotes— "a look, a smell of sandalwood and rain, cunnilingus, chalk hearts on pavements, silence," and that maybe the last hundred or two-hundred thousand years had produced a system that was in need of total overhaul. "*London Review of Books*," she says with a wave, "check it out." He says he will, which gives her a chance to come back to him, like the fabled detective Columbo used to do when talking to guilty people. She says, "I want to run the SE major. Honestly, it's what we do," meaning the creative writers. He wants to know what's in it for him. Her black eyes twinkle: "How would you like some pear cider from Zanzibar, bottled in 1956 by Donald Stravinsky?" Kenny whistles and shakes his dreads: must be a thousand a bottle. "If SE goes like I know it will, that, my friend, will be a drop in the bucket."

An adjunct with a criminal past, George Swan, is addressing a new intro class. He is doing so in the dark, while Harry Smith's *Heaven and Earth Magic* clouds the lens of the projector with its bizarre cut-out figures on a black background, and fills the room with found sounds: wolf howling, glass breaking, a watermelon being struck by a floating hammer and turning into a Victorian Woman in White, and so on.

"Your story has been told before. More than once. But you will venture your version here anyway, because, well, some of you have gone so far as to say you 'love writing'—and because we believe in the end that there is only one story to be told—by which we mean that stories that appear to have been authoritatively and satisfyingly told, must nevertheless, for some reason, be told again and again and again."

A complicated and ornate barber-chair explodes into a life of cantilevered engineering and pneumatic tubes as two cats snarl and spit.

"The Bible itself is just a latrine of willful mistranslations and bullshit commentary. There never has been and never will be more than one story to tell. The Buddhists speak of the ten thousand things, and it's true that the variations of the stories of things, just as the number of fools, is infinite, *that* story featuring *this*, *this* story featuring *that*, and mine featuring me, yours featuring you, variations, we say, of a species that all seem plainly and simply different, but the truth is that the genus, the family, the order, the class phylum kingdom, the domain where the bacteria and archaea and eukaryotes find distinction—these are all one with the deuterium and protium and quantum fluctuations of the Fragor Magnus."

Waves gently wash ashore. The floating hammer transforms a boy into a vegetable with tiny heads on each stalk or tuber, all spouting water.

"As it was in the beginning, as it is and ever shall be, infinite causes and conditions ceaselessly changing the story without end."

A head of a man, suggesting an eminent Edwardian physician whose jaw is unhinged, and who has been swallowing people, furniture, laboratory equipment, everything, has a hypodermic needle poked into his eyeball, which then distends, overwhelming the head, and is in turn worshipped by Gumby-like figures.

"You would think, too, wouldn't you, that there's nobody better to tell your story. But that is simply not true. You are not a reliable indicator of who you are and what you do. No one is. But I want you to tell me what you think it takes to be happy and succeed in life. That is the only assignment you will have for the entire semester. It must be at least a thousand words long."

The students, as one, move their eyes from their phones to their teacher.

One raises his hand, and when acknowledged, says, "You what?"

"A thousand."

"But—"

"One word for every dollar it costs to buy a bottle of

pear cider, bottled in 1956 in Zanzibar by Donald Stravinsky. I am told that at the end of the semester, to celebrate our work, we will all be taking a sip from just such a bottle."

"But—"

"Draw up a list, from a dictionary or TV shows, of words that attract you. We will workshop those words into sentences."

George tells them it will be easier than they think, and anyway, it's time to get the hell out of Dodge. Lions and tigers, numbers, two men in a boxing ring, and spiral shapes swirl around a ball, watched by dancing sarcophagi. A dog barks, water drips.

At home, George begins a slow and subtle process that will appear to age him from sixty to eighty by the end of the semester. He recalls long-forgotten guerilla theater techniques, in hopes of documenting just how hard Big Education is on adjuncts, but mostly just wants to see if anybody notices or cares.

Super Yin, who, out of uniform, has been mistaken countless times for Sojourner Truth, and Super Yang, who is often mistaken for Jackie Gleason, circle the equator twelve-thousand miles apart at a thousand miles an hour, one mile an hour for every dollar it costs to buy the pear cider favored by the gods. The former draws day in her wake, the latter night.

Controversy flares around the student newspaper. The creative writers, like single-celled organisms throbbing away from disturbance, seek to distance themselves from it, but because there are no journalism classes, they are departmentally in the thick of it: resistance journalism, perception management, it's all pretty creative, and it's really not that big a deal, as an adjunct actually teaches what passes for classes. But as little as the classes matter, the problem around the newspaper matters greatly. A very big donor, whose name is on buildings all over campus, has made a record-breaking contribution. The newspaper investigates, tries and fails to interview the president of the university, and runs a story in which it is suggested by an anonymous student that the scholarship will be awarded to white boys with entrepreneurial spirit. The Vice President for Student Life immediately dispatches her assistant, a former star student in the Creative Writing Department, whose evals were framed and hung in the departmental office as well as offered as templates for all majors, Denise Degas of the Las Vegas Degases, who dashes around campus and pulls all the copies from their racks because the donor is coming for a visit and pep-fest. She is seen looking this way and that for places to dump them, and awkwardly running here and there with her arms full. The conservative student body president calls emergency meetings to order day after exciting day, and succeeds in stripping the liberal newspaper of its funds. The newspaper's "professional advisor," an adjunct who is paid like an adjunct, i.e. at about two percent of the creative writers' salaries, is identified as the source of the libel: she is a black woman, and while that's circumstantial, to be sure, the reporter has confessed that she was prompted by the advisor to press the anonymous student for clarification. The clear but carefully implicit suggestion is that the black woman wanted to run down privileged white boys. Summarily relieved of her duties and instructed not to return to campus, the advisor wonders why nobody asked her for input. *That's democracy*, the wind whispers in the trees of the quad. *Simple, human responses compromise power and could very well leave you legally exposed*, she writes later, when faculty and admin

The Creative Writers

alike are secretly embarrassed to learn that she has become a Guest Essayist for the *New York Times*, where she writes about cowardice and the suppression of First Amendment rights on college campuses, as well as what she calls the cheerful racism of decent people.

The creative writers knew that the advisor was going through a particularly tough time in her life. Her increasingly violent and suicidal husband, against whom she had just begun divorce proceedings, went into the hospital for ulcer surgery, bled excessively, went into a coma, came out of it, was very confused, and died. Her dog died too. The hospital was quick to point out they'd handled everything perfectly, which turned out not to be true, and disclaimed all responsibility for the dog, who, the advisor believed, had pined excessively for her master. The creative writers acknowledged that it was a great story, but felt they could do nothing about it, as it wasn't material to her employment. And besides, the dean had asked them not to say anything about it, as talking would only make matters worse.

The Donald Ewen Cameron Chair for Young Adult Literature, Billy Greggs, in a devastating coup d'état to everything that was good and right in Title IX, succeeds in getting a friend of his hired as a campus-wide Sensitivity Trainer. Harry Lorenzo and Greggs had met on a panel at the Associated Writing Programs annual conference: "What You May Do and What You May Not Do: Sensitivity Readers and Desensitized Writers." The latter half had taken several hours, and by the end of the discussion, they had become ideological soulmates. So when Harry, a few months later, found himself hoist by his own explosive farting, with a book in which many faults of his own charting had been revealed, he needed a way to get more or less entirely out of literature, while maintaining his actionability skill-set, which featured his work on not talking about things.

Professor G, shuffling and slightly stooped, plays the familiar introduction to Carl Orff's *Carmina Burana*, the image a black screen with the Latin verses translated into English: "Oh, fortune! Like the moon you are changeable! Ever waxing and waning! Fate, monstrous and empty, turns your wheel. You are malevolent, wellbeing is vain and always fades to nothing. I bring my bare back to your villainy. Driven on and weighed down, always enslaved! So at this hour without delay, pluck the vibrating strings, since Fate strikes down the strong man, everyone weep with me!"

"You've heard the music a hundred times, in movies, TV commercials, sporting events—but I'm pretty sure you never knew what the lyrics were. Here's some more poetry from the medieval manuscript Orff based his work on. It's called *In the Tavern in Rage and Bitterness*. 'In rage and bitterness I talk to myself, made of matter, ash of the elements, I am like a leaf which the wind plays with. If a wise man builds his house upon a rock, I, fool, am like a gliding river which follows no straight path. I am swept away like a pilotless ship, like a bird floating aimlessly through the air. Jesting is lovely and sweeter than the honeycomb. On the broad road I move along as youth is wont to do. I am entangled in vice, and unmindful of virtue. Greedy more for lust than for welfare; dead in soul, I care only for my body.' This is the founding document for our class. As the aristocracy gradually moves out of The Dark Ages, from a state of more or less continuous war with each other to the Crusades and other wars with Muslims, knights find themselves increasingly out of work. These wandering knights are given full license to not only accomplish 'daring deeds of valor against the enmity of fiends' on behalf of 'fair maidens,' but to sing love songs to and in fact be in love with and attempt to seduce those fair maidens, who are actually the wives of kings, princes, dukes, barons. These knights, over the course of a couple hundred years, become court entertainers. They are called troubadours, a word that has a difficult derivation from roots in Provençal, Occitan, Latin, and Arabic, and means something like 'composer, finder, inventor.' With explosive population growth and the rise of towns and a merchant middle class, a second kind of entertainer emerges: *jongleurs* or minstrels. They are dismissed by the aristocratic troubadours as mere performers, rather than composers, but become extremely popular. As church and court continue to lose their grip on town life, and their monopoly on the arts, another group emerges: the *vagantes*: minstrel beggars, runaway priests, students who dropped out. Because the *vagantes* had no stake in established social and artistic order, they stripped away the romance and 'learnedness' from the court poets and began to develop a new kind of expression: naturalism. That is to say, they began to write and sing of the life around them as they found it, raw, vulgar, and real. They are, in effect, the distant ancestors of what we now call the Creative Writers. Do you see the *vagantes* in you? Do you see yourself in them? Can you make out any sort of connection at all? Or are they just Martian clowns from the Renaissance Festival. But let's go even further back."

Now there are images of prehistoric cave paintings on the screen. "The four horses of Chauvet, a masterpiece of world art, painted thirty thousand years ago. The wounded man of Lascaux. Look at him: the rhino and the bison are perfectly realistic, but he's not much more than a stick figure, wearing some kind of birdman helmet, holding a baton of commandment with another bird at the top, and sporting an enormous erection as the wounded bison, spilling its guts, charges him. Note the rhino: is he firing pellets of rhino shit at the man, or are those calendrical marks? Here is Altamira: one of the polychrome bulls that caused Picasso to say, 'After Altamira, all is decadence.' Here is the Cave of Three Brothers: the sorcerer or reindeer-god, the engraved grasshopper, the twenty-three-inch phallus, the therianthrope playing a nose-flute. Here's the Venus of Hohle Fels. We are looking at something *Homo sapiens* dreamed up and made out of nothing. There were no models, no precedents, no teachers, no tradition. They wanted to explore something in their minds that they couldn't account for. This thing had no name. We now call it art and science and religion, but in the beginning it was one thing and it had no name. It was theorized about around the campfire, and practiced as a means to...can anybody help me out? No? *They wanted to be happy and succeed in life.* Take the Wounded Birdman of Lascaux. What can we say about him?"

"He was some kind of leader?" Student X, who has fled Baltimore, asks.

Student Y, a mountaineer and rafting guide with a cigarette behind her ear and bangles everywhere, picks this up: "A shaman maybe?"

It is not lost on the class how shamanic Y's affect is.

"He was a big man in the Dordogne," says George, croaking and wheezing a bit. "Certainly. But what else?"

X takes a great leap. "He's about to die?"

Y proves she is a shaman. "And his imminent death is sexually exciting?"

"*Oui, tout cela est vrai.*" X and Y are the kind of students who actually make him feel young again. Their word hoards are well over a thousand, and, not accidentally, are the only two who, during a discussion of the precepts of positive psychology and the ways in which a person might be trained to be happy, voted against the proposition that torture of enemy combatants was acceptable if they had information that affected American lives.

"But what else?" Prof G continues. "Anybody? Nobody? Well, here's the thing: *he's unlucky.* He had it made, right? The easy-going but also quite exciting life of a hunter-gatherer, cooked food, the respect of his peers—but he's going to get gored by the bison, not the schmendrick who was standing next to him, who dropped his spear and ran for the cave."

"What's a schmendrick, professor?" asks X.

"An apprentice schlemiel."

Y is laughing now. "What's a schlemiel?"

"I am a Master Schlemiel. I usually wear a tall pointy cap and a grotesque codpiece. I lurk and dart as if everything surprises me. Look, say you two get drunk tonight. Shit-faced, you stumble into your automobiles and start to drive home. One of you sees a pedestrian trip off the sidewalk, and you just miss hitting him. But the other of you runs him over. The first continues to live the unblemished life of a public intellectual, while the second is punished and reviled. One of you will be happy and successful and one of you will not."

The class is silent.

"No, really now, how would that make you feel? Wouldn't that make you feel like you've been treated unfairly? There was no due process in the judgments, just dumb luck? Think about that: what's the fucking difference between you?"

Silence reigns supreme.

"Hit the lights."

Z, a big, sturdy woman with something of the reserve of a serious soldier, who has had her head on her arms from the beginning of class, rises slowly and switches the lights off. A video clip appears on the screen: Krishna counseling Arjuna in Peter Brook's adaptation of *The Mahabharata*. "Victory and defeat are the same. Act but do not reflect on the fruit of the act. Fight without desire. You must learn to see with the same eye the mound of earth and the heap of gold, a cow and a sage, a dog, and the man who eats the dog."

"Krishna is a god," asks X, "and Arjuna is like a superhero?"

"Krishna is the Hindu god of compassion, tenderness, and love."

"And he's wait, what?" Y interrupts. "Advising the greatest warrior on Earth to crank up a war that will...destroy civilization?"

"I don't get the good and evil here," X says, shaking his head and smiling ruefully. He leans back, tipping his chair onto its back legs: he doesn't get it now, but he feels good about the possibility of getting it in the near future.

"Don't think good and evil. Think yin and yang."

Super Yin and Super Yang suddenly appear, flanking George. Everybody sees them, but only in the way that images are imaged biochemically, with fire. They merge and begin slowly to spin around each other. They spin faster and faster, and grow larger and larger, until everyone in the classroom is spinning with them. Thanks to a quantum gyroscope, nobody senses the movement, but they all feel they have some intuitive understanding of yin and yang that they hadn't seconds earlier.

"Arjuna's nerve has failed him. All he has to do is make a decision, but he can't. Krishna is telling him he can't not make a decision: life forces us to act, and in fact, because all decisions are simply the confluence of an infinite number of causes and conditions, the decision has in effect already been made."

The swirling shapes and colors fade, and the spinning ceases.

"It's only in retrospect that we think we see freedom of will and independent decision-making. It's just Thought Number Ten in a never-ending series of reactive thoughts about 'what just happened.' Free will is the clown who gets the spotlight and takes the bow."

Y asks for clarification. "Free will is the clown who takes the bow?"

"Free will is a masturbation fantasy."

"Cool."

X asks for clarification. "Is it all right for us to be, you know, vulgar like that in our essay?"

"The Age of Gold is over. We live in the Age of Shit. The Age of Platinum Plus Bullshit. Vulgarity in the service of truth is bracing. Vulgarity in the service of lies is just diarrhea dribble on the crap-cake of mass mental illness."

"Professor," X says, "I'm still confused a little bit about the ultimate warrior and how the god of compassion's advice will make him happier."

"I am going to leap like a ballet dancer over your confusion and suggest that your real problem is the misperception of violence as meaningful entertainment. Is a massacre at a high school entertaining?"

"No."

"Is news coverage of the massacre entertaining?"

"No."

Y says, "Yes."

"Maybe," agrees X. "In a bad way."

"How about a movie in which CGI provides us with an up close and personal slaughter of thousands of evil people?"

"It's entertaining because it isn't real?"

"It's next to impossible to see the war between the cousin

princes of the Pandava and the Kaurava, and the descent of mankind from the Dvapara Yuga of truthfulness and compassion to the Kali Yuga of strife and discord as anything but a superhero blockbuster that gets suddenly overtaken by religious philosophy, right?"

"Yes, I think that's where I'm stuck."

"Why do people act violently?"

"They just do. Sometimes we can't help it."

"We don't know why. Most of the time, violence is just flat fucking inexplicable. It's irrational and unpredictable. It explodes. It does not, cannot, reckon consequences. The explosion of violence, even when it is feigned—this is important: even when it is feigned, on a stage or a screen or even in a classroom, it alters the fabric of reality. It disturbs and tears the fabric of the reality that we have so carefully built up around our fragile, mysterious selves, the reality that allows us to carry on with our plans for happiness and success. Our breathing changes, our heart rate increases, we feel overwhelming urges to either fight or flee. It takes our fragile sense of reality and holds it in suspension, so we can see what it was and how we can rebuild it. And 'build' is the word, because memory alone does not serve. It has been, at least momentarily, obliterated. If we are sure that the swords are electronic images that do not extend into three-dimensional space, or that the gun being fired on stage is loaded with blanks—and let's not forget that accident that propelled Christopher Marlowe to fame, when a pregnant woman enjoying the grandiloquence and bombast of his play *Tamburlaine* was killed—"

"Who's Christopher Marlowe, professor?" X asks.

"—then this act of destruction and rebuilding is exciting and pleasurable to watch. But if we are not sure how real the violence is, we peer down a long dark alley at the end of which we may glimpse psychosis: 'disorder in which thought and emotions are so impaired that contact is lost with external reality.'"

Y repeats X's question. "Who's Christopher Marlowe?"

"Contemporary of Shakespeare."

"A prop gun had live ammo in it? And killed someone in the audience?"

"Yes. It was a publicity stunt. Life was cheap back then, and publicity, then as now, was priceless and paramount."

Orgí, short, dark, and furious, and Alice, tall, cold, and judgmental, confront George when he passes their offices. They want to know what he thinks he's doing.

"Not teaching creative writing," he says. "I can assure you of that."

Unwilling, or more probably unable, to entertain irony and ambiguity, they tell him that that is exactly what he's been hired to do. But no. Instead he's showing his class lewd images of genitalia. Two CRWR major advisees have complained of such.

"Aubrey Beardsley's illustrations of Aristophanes's *Lysistrata,* and a terra cotta lamp in the shape of the god of the *phalloi*—"

"You are cruisin' for a bruisin', mister," says Alice.

"And here comes Muhammad Alice. Clearly not the fighter she once was, but still able to rhyme. Thanks for the tip, Champ! Say, did you know that our class flag features the famous photo of Ali snarling over Liston, with a speech bubble coming from Liston saying, 'Life a funny thing. People strange. I'd rather be a lamppost in Denver than the mayor of Philadelphia.' I wanted another image, of Ali shitting on George Frazier for marketing purposes, but I'm not very good with computers."

As if they are in a musical, Alice and Orgí toss their heads in synch, enter their offices, and slam the doors. It's all George can do to keep from singing.

Ike Perlmutter, Chairman of Marvel Entertainment, Trump campaign megadonor, Mar-a-Lago companion, and de facto head of the VA, visits campus and grabs Super Yin and Super Yang by the backs of their necks. He has decided that their superpower, to inexorably and ceaselessly transform one universal binary into the other, is inimical to the practice of power. The stark opposition of good and evil and the consequent generation of fear is particularly important. But what he really wants, he whispers to Yang, is to do away with Yin once and for all: complete and unchangeable domination of the streets of the mind. After he's done hollering at his heroes, he meets secretly with the creative writers. They tell him it's in the bag. Jackie Gleason in the ring with Sojourner Truth? They're going to have to work hard to make it look even a little close. Ike alerts Big Gambling and the stage is set for the one percent of the one percent of the one percent to run the table and move to Mars.

G Tha Proffet produces a pie crust from his backpack. He shuffles slowly around the room, showing it to the students with comic gestures that he says are derived from vaudeville and commedia dell'arte. He has been wearing a series of bald caps with less and less hair on them, and beards that are whiter, wispier, and longer. He wears huge glasses that magnify his eyes, and often pauses to catch his breath. Today he is wearing a beanie with a propeller on top.

"This is an ancient Italian stage joke, or *lazzo*. I'm going to pretend to get angry, and threaten to smash the pie in one of your faces."

He produces a can of Redi-Whip and fills the crust with it. He is a clown-chef, and he circles the class again, proud of his pie.

"I make a big, very elaborate *lazzo* out of selecting my target for the pie."

He stands before Z, who sits up, stiffens, looks alarmed and confused.

"Then I make the biggest *lazzo* of all as I suddenly pretend to be angry and say GODDAMMIT I'M SICK OF YOU ALL SLEEPING THROUGH MY LECTURES AND NOT UNDERSTANDING WHAT I'M TALKING ABOUT! Now I wind up and prepare to smash the pie in Z's alarmed and confused face."

He hovers the pie near Z's face, who is frozen. He moves it away, jolts it forward, pulls it back, sails it around like a comic waiter.

"Now everybody in the audience—that's you in this case, a collection of scholars the like of which this university hasn't seen for decades—is wondering, 'Is he really going to do this? Is he really going to do what he's warned us he's going to do?'"

He tenses as if he's about to deliver the pie to Z's face, then suddenly lunges at X, who falls over backward in his chair. Super Yin and Super Yang reappear, trembling on the edge of substantiality, as X collects himself and the nervous laughter dies down.

"It's horrifying and hilarious, is it not? To see cruelty exposed and the machinery of laughter and make-believe evaporate?"

"Okay, yes," says Y. "That was interesting, but you're going to have to walk us through what that has to do with how to be happy and succeed in life, I think."

"Violence, even when feigned—put your phones

down, do not call 911—changes the atmosphere, changes brainscapes, changes physiognomy, changes, for all intents and purposes, reality. Nobody saw coming what I just did, even though I told you that I was going to do it, and you all had to recalibrate instantly your sense of the room. We were talking about how violence interferes with success and happiness, and we just saw how that can happen, even though it was a *lazzo*, a bit of silly stage violence. Violence seems unavoidable in our world. Our responses to it are what matters. We must oppose with all our might the soft-headed tolerance of and insistence on banality and nothing-at-stake pseudo-emotionality, the intellectual and spiritual bad camouflage of so-called creative writing. Creative writing is destroying American literature. I want you to make art that makes people lose their bearings and tip over, just like Baltimore X did. Your happiness is being interfered with on a scale of violence so massive it doesn't even register as violence, which we all helplessly associate with slaps and kicks and bites, and guns held close to the face of the hero, and cool explosions that waft those heroes up and away to safety rather than sunder them at the atomic level. Have you noticed how much the creative writers here seem to want to be your friend, and help you with your personal life? That's because they're really not your friend. They despise you and make fun of you behind your backs. Some of you may know CW majors, and seen the gift baskets they have been given as graduation presents. They get those baskets because there's always a little left over in the departmental purse and instead of giving you books we give you swag, like a tote bag full of luxury toothbrushes when you buy a car. You're a customer, not a student, not a writer, and truth be told, most of you don't even like to read. That disqualifies you as a writer, but we are creativity profiteers and it's far more important that we bribe you and tell you about the benefits of being part of a community of writers than give you a book, say, that proves you have been a victim of a hoax and defrauded you of what, $200,000? And put you in debt for life? Do you know why you've been beaten and imprisoned in this way? Do you know why we spent so much time talking about how happiness can be forced on you? DO YOU KNOW WHAT THE SEVEN BREAKTHROUGH SOLUTIONS ARE? Jeez, now I'm really angry, kids. But look what happens: just as with Amba in *The Mahabharata*, 'anger keeps me young.'"

George takes a jar of cold cream from his backpack, turns his back on his students, wipes off all the old-man makeup, pulls the bald cap and false beard off, and spins back to face the class, shouting TA-DA! He straightens his spine and throws back his formidable shoulders. They gasp, and a couple of them actually jump up from their seats. A phone, then, two, then three clatter to the floor. Jaws bang on the table. He looks even younger than they do. He declares that he has been transformed, and is being given a second chance.

"You can only succeed in life if you accept *their* happiness."

George and Alice and Orgí and Harry and Billy are arranged around a low, conversation-enhancing table in Kenny B Dean's office. The dean doesn't want to rush to judgment—he steeples his fingers—but he does have to move quickly, as George's class meets again tomorrow. This is the opportunity to comment.

"On what."

"It must be pretty clear to you."

"Nobody's told me a thing. I have no idea what's going on."

"You know very well what happened."

"You are either conflating or are simply confused by the difference between my presence in the classroom and knowledge of my offense."

"There was a disturbing incident."

"I'm aware of all the incidents, as you suggest, but the disturbing part has yet to get its boots on the ground."

No one says anything. No one moves. Super Yin appears subliminally and begins to play a recording of Charles Ives's *The Unanswered Question*. The first bars are like the opening music for *Star Trek*, just before Kirk starts mugging and the sexy 60s adventure music cranks up. Ives called this nearly unvarying set of ground notes "The Silence of the Druids." Everyone can hear it but nobody remarks it. The dean unsteeples.

"Are we talking," asks George, "about the discussion and demonstration of *commedia dell'arte*?"

"Tell us about that."

"No. I'd like you to tell me about that."

The Silence of the Druids continues.

"Are you telling me that I have been secretly denounced? Excuse me: are you *not* telling me that I have been secretly denounced?"

A lonely trumpet plays the five plaintive notes that represent the unanswered question, but hears no reply.

"And that I may not—must not—know the charges against me? Or the identity of my accuser? Or hear evidence against me? Have an advocate?"

"I," says Alice, "am your advocate."

"I'd like a real advocate, not some John Cage-inspired non-advocate." This is a reference to trips Alice makes to a little church in Germany where a continuously playing note, inspired by Cage, is changed every five years, and her devotion to blank canvas, silent music, immobile dance, and junk sculpture.

Largo molto sempre. Then suddenly the discordant woodwinds, which Ives called "The Fighting Answerers," as if they were wearing racoon coats and straw hats and holding pennants. Their shrill burst of frustration is represented in the room by Kenny squeaking hoarsely that they don't want to rush to judgment. The sharply rising inflection at the end gives the dean's anxiety away: they do want to rush to judgment, they have already rushed to judgment, but the whole thing depends on staying cool and appearing to be not rushing to judgment. He drops his gaze in shame because everybody knows now that he is afraid of something. He starts to say that something has crossed his mind, but says it has crossed his head—and he just stops. Everyone stares at him. They are seeing the thought making its way through his dreads.

O lost, thinks George. O simple and human, lost!

Harry the suave Sensitivity Trainer assumes the posture and tone of a disinterested friend of fair inquiry. "Could you describe the cream-pie business to me? I don't quite understand what it has to do with Creative Writers."

"Not to mention," says Billy, as if he imagined himself to be Gore Vidal being interviewed on the Dick Cavett Show, "your collection of paleo-erotica, the nonsense movie you have playing during the entirety of every class—"

"It's not nonsense. It's non-nonsense for a non-fiction workshop. They are symbols of the real struggling against the enemies of the real."

"May I finish? May I? Thank you. May I? And the psychodrama, which ceased to be fashionable forty years ago, and was generally understood to be nothing more than a chance to shout fuck you at invisible loved ones."

"It wasn't psychodrama, Gore. Now I'm going to punch you in the nose like Norman Mailer did."

Sad but knowing looks all around. This reckless truculence is precisely what they are trying to get at.

"Does this all have something to do," asks the Dunning-Kruger Chair of Creative Effort, "with the aging Neanderthal comedian thing you had going on until…until whatever you have going on now? Which is what exactly? Cosmetic surgery? Frankly I think you look scary and weird and I'm sure more than one student felt the same way."

"If we are in fact talking about the cream-pie *lazzo*, I must say that the class responded enthusiastically to the point I was trying to make."

"Obviously," says Alice coolly, almost demurely—again, a signature—almost primly, "not the whole class."

"I think you'll agree," says the Sensitivity Trainer, "that one damaged student is more important than ten who responded enthusiastically."

"'Damaged student'?"

"Re-traumatization is a very serious business. There's not a whole lot of wiggle room."

"'Re-traumatization'? 'Wiggle room'? Oh wait, I see, I see: if I was a tenured prof there would in fact be wiggle room, but because I am a temp worker getting paid $3000 a semester, there is not? O, lost, the democracy of the common man! *Who is damaged? What is the nature of the trauma and how was the damaged person retraumatized?*"

The strings providing the ground note go up a note, then down a note, as super Yin and Super Yang produce their conducting batons and begin fencing with them. The trumpet makes its mournful cry. The woodwinds shriek in anger. Super Yin whispers something unintelligible to George, who makes a face.

"Can one of you tell me why the simple, ordinary, human solution to this problem was not pursued? One that has me being told what happened, me apologizing, several of us talking it out, all of us emerging wiser and friendlier than before?"

"Questions of legal exposure," says Alice, "outweigh all other considerations."

"We've been friends for years, Alice."

"Questions of legal exposure outweigh all other considerations, particularly loyalty to friends."

"'Fear,' I quote the *New Left Review* as closely as I can remember, 'of legal exposure results in craven overcompliance.'"

"Questions of legal ex—"

The disembodied voice of Ike Perlmutter crackles like thunder from the phone on Kenny's desk: "QUESTIONS OF LEGAL EXPOSURE OUTWEIGH ALL OTHER CONSIDERATIONS PERIOD!"

Kenny is hyperventilating now, and mops his brow. Alice leans back in sober triumph. The late comedian Bill Hicks appears before George, like Christ, ironically, in a sinner's hour of need. This must be what Super Yin was whispering about. Bill is very cool, beatific in fact, wearing sunglasses, a leather jacket, and smoking a cigarette. He offers one to George, who takes it. Bill lights it up for him. All anybody else can see is a smoky light around George's head like a halo. Bill feeds George his lines.

"Well! Thank you! Thank you very much! It's great to be here in Redlands, where the high desert meets the low desert. Which is kind of a misnomer, don't you think? The low desert, correct me if I'm wrong—but don't get upset if I bite your fucking tiny heads off because, hey, I know more about everything than you do, all right? I know you think you're 'scholars,' right? Very smart people, the cream of the smart crop. Let's twist the dial and see if we can get—here we are. [imitates static and radio announcer] 'What's the price today for a bushel of smarts? Oh gee, that's not so good. That low? Really? I guess China is flooding the market with cheap smarts, and, let's see here, Russia! Russia's efforts to make everyone more stupid—making the cheapest smarts look like luxury goods—are really paying off as well. Doesn't look good for intelligence in the U.S.A.' All right. Well, that's bad, but looks like we're going to be all right in this room. You people are so smart it's making my eyes water. What was I saying? Oh yeah: the particularly arid quality of this region. The brittle and desiccated brains of the organisms that live here. The low or Sonoran Desert is where you get those crazy dudes eating peyote and flying, right? [imitates Fleetwood Mac song] 'Seems like a dream, they got me hypnotized.' Instead of taking the bus: 'Jesus Christ, man, can you please not piss on my shoes?' Nope. No way. You take the bus and you get some guy lying down in the aisle and pissing up like he thinks he's a fucking fountain, a work of art—No. No way, man. The people of the low desert, they just…*get high, man*. And examine their minds for traces of soul, and confront the evil in themselves. Those crackling weightless brains just get sopping wet with the juice of life, man. The fucking *elixir* of the fucking *gods*, man. Now would any of you like to get high with me? No? Really? No? Well I can't say I'm surprised. You're smart, you're altruistic, you're just looking to apply market forces to higher ed. [imitates stoner] Ed? Who's Ed? Dude can't be higher than me. I don't believe it. No one can be higher than me, man. I have examined my mind for traces of soul AND HAVE ACTUALLY FOUND SOME! I have confronted the evil in myself and while I have found a great deal of evil, I have to say, folks, that it is NOTHING compared to the arid, dead-eyed fountains of bloody urine WHOOSH SPLATTER WHOOSH SPLATTER OH MY GOD I'M DYING WHO CAN I KILL BEFORE I GO and wormy bullshit in this room. SEVEN BREAKTHROUGH SOLUTIONS? SOLUTIONS TO WHAT? Were people like, learning too freely or something? Were they reading and writing and thinking for themselves? Breakthrough Solution Zero: offer students membership in your weird, sick little cult of market forces and machine-gun everybody who doesn't accept! Who needs 'em? If they don't want to be part of a better tomorrow, let the vultures of the high desert have them! The straight-arrow vultures of the high desert and the super high vultures of the low desert. Isn't that kinda sweet, though? A genuinely pleasant thought? Sister Vulture, Brother Vulture, here, this is my body, take of it and eat. When two or three of you gather in my name, eat me in remembrance of me. Drink my blood and eat my flesh. That sounds right, doesn't it? Properly religious?"

The others in the room are making clear signs of impatience and frustration, but something is holding them in stasis. Every once in a while a snarling bark, faint and staticky, can be heard coming from the phone, Ike the P demanding Super Yang get his shit together, and telling Super Yin to stop if she wants to keep her job.

Bill/George puts on a goober yokel voice. "Shoot, here's a problem. Teachers ain't neither efficient nor effective. Hit's takin' way too long to download the job skill stuff and lookee here, sometimes they just yawnin' and scratchin' they asses with history and philosophy, which never got nobody nowhere nohow. [interrupts himself] Why don't you just shut the fuck up and fuck the hell off. And instead of dividing the costs of professors' salaries and benefits by the number of students they teach, ranking faculty by cost-per-student taught, comparing student satisfaction ratings with grade distributions, collecting and reading all research articles for high-cost faculty, and publicly posting information on student ratings and number of students taught—why don't you just reverse the whole fucking thing and make professors pay the students. That would make them the customers and as you've been saying, the customer is always right. The professor could notice that a student hasn't shown up for class, denounce them, and BOOM they'd be gone! Clear out your desk and security will see you out. Professors could have their own student-ranking website, and soon enough, you'd have thousands of students that no professors are willing to teach! And here, where you're awarding bonuses of up to $10,000 per class to the best teachers based on student evaluations and number of students taught, including all faculty ranks: professors, lecturers, adjuncts and teaching assistants, and awarding up to $10,000 bonuses to the top 3 percent of teachers, and prizes of up to $5,000 to the rest of the top 10 percent and $2,500 to the rest of the top 25 percent, why don't you just set up a deal where profs are offering small cash rewards to anybody who'll sign up for their class, and further small cash rewards for positive evals, and run all that through a computer, with the prof who has the greatest number of students and the greatest number of positive evals as a kind of winner-take-all, zero-sum conclusion? Everything's zero-sum, right? Even four-way stops are zero-sum: WHOEVER GOES FIRST, WINS! EVERYBODY ELSE—LOSES! And maybe a lottery for the profs who lose, so they don't get discouraged! They'd all get minimum wage jobs, too, of course, janitorial and so on, or working in the food-appropriation courts, where black markets offering no-no items like sushi and burritos and spaghetti could provide decent livings. Now let's move on to Breakthrough Solutions Three through Seven—"

Here is where Super Yang/Jackie Gleason, who has been choking and beating Super Yin/Sojourner Truth, finally gets the upper hand. Ike howls in a kind of miniature computer voice for Yang to finish her off. But no: Yin and Yang being who they are, Yin slowly turns the table on Yang. This allows George to finish his presentation.

"*Well,*" he says. "This has been fun, but you know what? It just so happens that I can..."

He reaches into his backpack and produces a cream pie.

"...produce the murder weapon and recreate, right here and now, all the comic *lazzi* before your very eyes, the whole disturbing, damaging, re-traumatizing incident! Now remember: I'm telling you what I intend to do, and telling you that I'm not going to do it, just to demonstrate how alarming even fake, comic violence can be disturbing and disruptive—even as it entertains."

He pulls the fingertips of his left hand together and places the pie atop them. With his right hand he takes off with a flourish an imaginary hat, throws out his left leg, and swings his free arm high and wide, the downward arc of which guides a bow such as Molière might have instructed his troupe to use, head almost to the knee, pie held high. He straightens, then makes the faintest lunges perceptible, little more than widenings of the eye, toward each of the other three.

"No? No? No?" Using his theatrically trained baritone, he sings "WHICH OF YOU WILL WIN THE JOSEPH STALIN PRIZE FOR SECRET TRIALS AND SUMMARY EXECUTION? Aw fuck it, I'll just ask my friend to write an op-ed about all this in the *New York Times*. See ya!"

Super Yin lofts George to Hollywood while Super Yang

does a slow-burn and Ike Perlmutter's rage causes the whole of the university's phone system to explode.

The NDA is revealed to be about, at least in part, a substantial change to employment contracts: forced arbitration. Faculty sign away their right to sue and must never speak of it. The dean, the provost, and the president hire bodyguards. The creative writers focus on coming of age tales set in fairyland. Until, in one of the fits of pique the president of the university has come to enjoy indulging in as his power and corruption near the absolute, he lambastes all the huddled professors of humanities, demanding to know what the fuck they had that he could sell—and it is here that the creative writers unveil their plans for both a Master of Creativity program and a major in Spiritual Entrepreneurship. Included are: Techniques of Outreach and Perception Management for Creatives, Community Arts fairs, summer classes for grade-school kids in which, for example, students would be asked to come up with their favorite line in a movie or TV show and then to write it down, classes in Business and Arts Administration, and Digital Arts.

Most importantly, this coincides with the concatenative publication of Alice Reznya's international blockbuster *Seven Words*, which are *music, bread, woman, dog, I, you,* and *weather*, each on its own page, and each conjuring new images every time they are glanced at. It goes viral and spawns countless imitations, but readers by and large want the real thing, the genuine article, cloth bound, and it sells hundreds of thousands of copies, advertising along the way the new programs for which ten new adjuncts are hired, at a total cost of $60,000 a year, making its profit margin, as calculated by the AWP, tops by far. Orgí catches the wave and during the next year publishes two books, *The Write Space: Home Re-hab for Creatives* (be friendly but firm with the help, because just like housemaids who don't dust underneath the *objet d'art*, contractors will use as few nails as they can get away with) and *Pay It Forward: Estate Planning for Creatives*, which opens up a completely new curriculum dealing with intellectual property and legal exposure. They both win Shmulitzers—upsetting a decade-long regime that had seen two writers trading the prize—and MacFarthurs. The president of the university calls the creative writers into his office and hands them a big "Styrofoam Key to the Campus." But they are already eying off-campus real estate development—a largely fraudulent operation being run by former Star Student in the CRWR, Denise Degas of the Las Vegas Degases (a cabal of construction czars), whose framed evals of her profs are hung in the department office and also used as templates for current students looking for help in praising their teachers, an able and ambitious young woman who, thanks to private CRWR dough, was elected to the Redlands City Council—and they are beginning to find the dean, the provost, and the prez…a little pathetic.

2

In which a video surfaces of tuxedoed cyclists racing from Santa Monica to Hollywood for the Oscars. A fatal accident in that race ties George Swan to Frederick Funston IV, a movie mogul. They become Brothers in Art.

Frederick Funston the Fourth is the great-grandson of Frederick Funston the First, after whom the street in San Francisco is named. Fred Four is a movie producer who went to college and law school with the former president of the United States, Harry Mo'bama. He is in his small, plain, humbly furnished and undecorated office on San Vicente, in the Barry Building, a run-down set of shops and offices in two stories around an open courtyard in the California Mid-Century Modern style. The first-floor shops are all part of a bookstore: if you want to leave Fiction and browse History, you have to leave one musty shop and pass through the palm-treed courtyard to another. There are books everywhere, three deep on mismatched shelves, floor to ceiling in narrow aisles, spilling everywhere. As if part of a natural buildup, there are books all over Fred's office upstairs, too. He's talking to John Fellows, a highly reputable political writer, who had written speeches for Billy Jack Carter, most notably the one that pardoned Vietnam draft-dodgers, and the one about the installation of solar panels for the White House. It's the late Indiana senator Birch Buy, however, for whom he campaigned as a teenager, that Fellows wants to pitch as the subject of a bio-pic: a man for all legislative seasons, one of the architects of the Civil Rights Act, tireless campaigner for the Equal Rights Amendment and the abolition of the electoral college—he even saved Ted Threnody's life after a plane crash. When Fred brings up Mo'bama's reinterpretation of the CRA's Title IX, the "Dear Colleague" letter that had unleashed people like Harry Lorenzo, John recalls a conversation he had with a teacher who had been fired from a university in his hometown, on the board of which he had sat for a brief while. The firing, as far as John could see, wasn't a Title IX case, i.e., having to do with sexual poison, but had been treated as such. It was hard to say for sure, because secrecy was its main condition, and he had tried to attract an editor at *The Pacific* with a broader tale of degeneracy in Higher Ed, but to no avail. The teacher had shown him another story, about his time on Shore Patrol in the Philippines and its rather attenuated conclusion in an incident of pre-PTSD PTSD featuring an Army Ranger who'd been a part of the invasion of Grenada. Fred says he'll read the stories. But when John leaves, he chooses instead to watch something that has just come in over his intelligent-phone.

It's a blurred and jerky video of a bike race, apparently taken by one of the racers, or riders, racing being perhaps too strong a word for what was really just a celebration of new biking laws in Los Angeles. But as he watches it, he is reminded of the Zapruder film.

There are his hands, on the bar of his bicycle. Cut to his friends massed around him, all wearing tuxedos, pumping furiously. They are on their way to the Oscars. Cut to the windows of the fashionable shops blurring past, a miles-long expanse of dark glass through which only ghosts can be seen, their eyes appearing and disappearing, as if in a super-fast-motion time-lapse recording of the universe. There are the small groups of shoppers pausing to take in the whirring mass. Cut to someone else's hand on his handlebar. Cut to the Captain America-helmeted head of his arch-nemesis

Vincent Gorbo. He's known the fringe conspiracist Gorbo since he and Gorbo and Mo'bama were all students at Occidental in Eagle Rock. Gorbo's very large head veers sharply away. Cut to the massive grill, bumper, and blue fender of a Pacific Gas and Electric truck. The only sound on the video is the powerful burning of oxygen, the microphone deep in someone's lungs.

The sunset is one of the most beautiful he has ever seen: deep orange just as it's about to become red like the wall of a wildfire, ink-black shapes of buildings and trees with even the smallest network of twig and leaf sharp and fine, sharper and finer than any pen ever made could draw, no bleeding, no flaring—etched with a diamond on glass so that each object looks as if could be pressed from its plate and hung as a decoration on the bracelet slung around the trunk of the palm at the end of the mind. The orange-red higher in the sky is mixed with washes of faint pink and charcoal-bottomed gray clouds. But it is the blue that makes the sky seem a work of fantasy. It's a blue he has never seen in the sky before, and will never see again: something like a baby blue but impossibly dense with pigment—or rather, because it seems painted rather than naturally occurring, it is the blue of a glazed ceramic bowl in which the paint has saturated the whole, making it—he thinks of Wallace Stevens and Henri Michaux—the solid of blue.

Cut to the Captain America head, the blue and white in a puddle of red that seeps into the map-like lines of the cracked blocks of deteriorating asphalt, eyes staring in fear and hatred with the light that had made them menacing now quite departed. He was briefly accused of causing Gorbo's death, but nothing had come of it.

In which movie projects are discussed and some personal history is revealed, suggesting George and Fred were destined to meet by forces beyond human ken. Another video clip adumbrates horror to come.

3

Another video is being filmed at the University of Redlands. It's part of the promotional effort for the new programs. It's a professional production and is running way over a budget that was big to begin with. There are many scenes, ranging from a tour of the University library's archives, featuring handwritten notes on workshopped manuscripts from the earliest days of the department, with grainy black and white photographs of those same workshops, to stop-motion animations of students writing in palm trees. Another scene is called Student Care, and recreates the episode that terminated George Swan's contract. Student Z plays herself. It's followed by a lively, engagingly humorous but serious panel discussion of the lengths to which the University will go to protect students from teachers. Creativity being what it is, they are willing to entertain the possibility of doing without teachers altogether, with supervision from afar and an enhanced FAQ suite of tools.

Fred Funston invites George Swan to the Barry Building for a chat. George, getting out of his car, sees a man he takes to be Fred, waving at him and gesturing at the sky. He turns and see a small plane very low to the ground and coming more or less straight at him.

In the slowly evaporating marine layer of the Los Angeles afternoon sky, across the little postage stamp of a parking lot, leaflets in a cloudy whirl are drifting down. Countenancing in all sobriety an image of himself as a screenwriter, in just the way Stanislavski suggested an actor prepares, builds a character, and creates a role—his famous ABC of acting—and staring at the blizzard of flyers, George isn't paying attention to where he's going and steps in a pile of shit. Because there are so many handy, he grabs a flyer to wipe it off. But before he can apply it to his worn-out sneaker, he reads the note:

FEARLESS FREDDIE FUNSTON THE FOURTH IS A FUCKING FRAUD!

There is a mural on the wall outside Fred's office. The wall is plaster over bricks, painted light blue. The plaster has cracked in places, exposing the brown brick. The mural is a picture of a person painting a mural on a wall of brick and cracked plaster. The mural wall is darker blue plaster over red bricks. The person is halfway up a ladder, holding a piece of paper on which is what looks like a sketch of the mural being painted. Back to the viewer, the painter is staring at the sketch in one hand, while with the other, arm stretched out nearly straight, he darkens a preliminary line. The object being painted is a human brain, as wide as the person is tall. The artist's name is Lucy McKenzie.

In the office, they get to know each other, and much is made of their having passed each other by twenty years earlier and never known it. It was in New York, around Union Square, where Fred was producing his first movie, *Rebel Gurl*, about the life of Elizabeth Gurley Flynn, and George was selling review copies at the Strand Bookstore. An actor George had known from his nights in the theater in Minneapolis in the 80s had accosted him as he lugged his box of books past a line of semi-truck trailers and motorhomes. As they'd talked, the actor had waved and shouted at a man he called Freddie. George had been working on a novel about anarchists at that time. The name Freddie Funston had caused more researches to be undertaken. It in fact opened up a new vein, which led to a mother lode of news about a subject he thought he had well in hand but which he knew next to nothing about.

"I know quite a lot about your great-grandfather, Fearless Freddie. The street in San Francisco is named after him." He places his hand on the pocket of his jeans and hears the thick crinkle of the leaflet. "And Fearless Teddy Roosevelt. The Spanish-American War, The Philippine-American War. The Earthquake and Fire of '06, and the Regenerators. The Golden Age of Graft and the Golden Age of Graft Prosecution. Jack Pershing and Pancho Villa. Emma Goldman, Leon Czolgosz, Alexander Berkman and Henry Clay Frick, Mooney and Billings and the Preparedness Day Bombing. The IWW and the Watchdogs of Loyalty. It was General Funston who ordered the black powder firebreak explosions during the earthquake and fire of 1906. Which caused, they say, more fires than they stopped. And he ordered his soldiers to shoot looters on sight. Which caused, it is believed, the deaths of many innocent people."

"You have to ask the questions first. If you don't, if you just go ahead and shoot, it's one of these classic travesties of justice that we are always hearing so much about."

"Maybe there's a movie there too. Not for me, of course, but some other big shot with money."

"Why not you? Why not a movie about Funston in the Philippines and Frisco? There's your title: *Fearless Freddie Funston, the Filipino Franciscan*. Or *Apocalypse Now: 1901*."

"Well, there is a movie about the Philippines I'd like to make, but it isn't a war movie, and I kinda have to wait to see how some litigation I'm involved in falls out."

"I'd like to make a movie about the Pillapeens, too."

Fred is standing at the window, looking at the parking lot.

"Dropping leaflets from a Piper Cub. It's crazy. You know my father used to fly around with this other blacklisted guy and dump anti-McCarthy leaflets on Beverly Hills? Said he also took shits over Orange County."

Fred and George find themselves jammed impossibly behind the two seats of the little airplane. Fred's father, Fearless Freddie the Third, who is just Fred Four with a pencil-thin moustache, is wiping his ass with a leaflet. Over the roar of wind and engine, he shouts:

"Hope a dingleberry survives the fall and lands in somebody's martini! 'Manuel! I told you to hold the olives!' 'Wow!' says Manuel. 'That's some olive!'"

Fred and George watch from the cockpit as leaflets funnel downwards and land in the tiny parking lot outside the tiny Barry Building. At some point the cockpit window again becomes the office window, from which they both turn, decisively, only to feel that decisiveness swallowed up in a fog of unease. Another video is delivered to Fred's phone, and both men watch it.

The camera on the helmet jerks and wobbles this way and that: the pink and grey sky, green awnings over shop fronts, blurred cheering people on the sidewalks, food trucks, car traffic stopped at intersections, heads poking out windows, arms and hands in esoteric gestures, and its microphone picks up honking horns and panting lungs and whirring tires: it certainly looks like a festive bicycle race. But half of the cyclists—the helmet-cammed rider passes them as if they are standing still—are dressed in tuxedos and half look like bulge-muscled superheroes. But if the action is slowed, the blurry people come instantly into focus: an old woman in a lace cap with her eyes rolled up in her head, a skeleton wearing purple pajamas and a human mask, a man wearing a navy blue top hat whose nostrils are at the end of a long snout and whose eyes are black ellipses cut in some kind of wrinkled cloth, a big baby who looks like a doll holding a doll that looks like a baby, a Beefeater Guard wearing a skeleton mask and holding a woman in a wedding dress with nothing but a great curving beak for a face framed by a halo-like lace cap, a woman wearing a shapeless yellow sack, tiny round blue-tinted sunglasses, and smears of red lipstick on a mouth that stretches from ear to ear.

The camera searches the racers, flicking right and left, the wearer's own breath becoming louder and more pained. At last the camera wobbles and shakes and seizes on Vincent Gorbo, who is pumping madly and shouting incoherently.

"DADDY!" shouts the camera-wearer: a young girl's voice.

The camera jerks and finds Fred, who is pumping madly too, and shouting.

"FUCK OFF YOU FUCKING FASCIST FREAK!" shouts Fred.

"PARTY OF LINCOLN, ASSHOLE!" shouts Daddy.

Fred fends off a grab for his handlebars, and gives Daddy Gorbo a shove back, hitting his shoulder. Gorbo veers sharply off. Tires screech and horns blare. The camera falls to the asphalt, remains as motionless as if dead for a second or two, then struggles upright. It sees Gorbo lying under his mangled bike, limbs at sickening angles, the tarmac seething. The camera sees bleary faces of frightened grotesques.

"Daddy! Daddy! Daddy! Don't die! DADDY!"

"I…I…I love you, sweetie…."

"Oh Daddy I love you too! Daddy no! Don't die Daddy!"

The camera sees Super Yin and Super Yang begin to swirl around Gorbo. The other people vanish. Gorbo vanishes in swirls of deepening darkness. The darkness becomes an empty highway in the desert, the swirls lighter now, a swirling light that envelops the fallen and mangled Fred. Many years have apparently passed, and he looks much, much older.

"That's not," the ancient Fred whispers, bubbling blood, "how it happened."

A man Fred can't see says, "What's not how what happened."

"That's not how he died."

"That's not how who died."

"Him."

"Who him."

"I never shoved him. I swatted his hand away."

"Swatted whose hand away?"

"The dead guy. He was fucking with me."

The flashing lights of a cop car and an ambulance bathe Fred in alarming light. He is loaded into the ambulance.

In which Super Yin and Super Yang, out of costume and manifesting as agents, begin to vie for the right to represent George, who has changed his name back to the original Finnish, Joutsen. Personal histories of the Philippines: Fred's great-grandfather, a general in the Philippine-American War of 1898, and George, a sailor during the Vietnam War.

4

There is the Earth, the blue pearl in velvet space. This is, the people of Earth believe, the only place in the infinite universe that knows the universe exists. There are the lights of the great cities, where profit from this knowledge is managed. The planet is slowly spinning, at about a thousand miles an hour: lights are slowly extinguished, one by one, as daylight advances, then flare up again, one by one until they number in the trillions, as darkness swallows up the day. There is Super Yin, her white suit glowing in the darkness as she pursues Super Yang in his black suit, shining in the daylight.

And there is Super Yin in her office, which is empty, save a few cardboard boxes, a card table and folding chairs, loops of unconnected cables and cords, a broom, a dustpan, and a large wheeled curbside trash bin, a silver and green wig, and two very old, very small men in tuxedos, hunched over a harmonium and a harpsichord, both instruments of music ornately carved and extravagantly painted pieces of outré furniture. They are playing six short works for two keyboards by Antoni (Francisco Javier Jose) Soler i Ramos, a Catalan monk-mathematician who flourished just as the Baroque was giving way to the Classical. The choice of keyboards, the clickety-whirring virginal and the wheezy-piercing pump organ, is odd but charming. Many of the padre's keyboard works are positively cheery, and the first concerto sounds very much, even when played on grand pianos, like something you might hear on a carousel. Add the calliope-like tone, and put it in a small empty industrial space with heavy sun-blocking curtains over the windows, and the reader has in hand the once-mighty Yin Talent Agency.

Fred, still troubled by his bad dream of the desert highway in the future, climbs exterior, motel-like stairs to the second floor, and enters an unmarked metal door. The hallway goes on and on and on in both directions, and there are no side offices. At one end, to his right, just barely visible but somehow as sharply focused as a butterfly under a magnifying glass, a black door with a white *taijitu* on it. To his left, equally far away and equally distinct, a white door with a black *taijitu* on it.

The doors come off their hinges and start to move slowly toward each other, taking up the whole hallway, floor to ceiling, wall to wall. They pick up speed, then crash into each other, like the supreme binary that yin and yang toss into the maelstrom, past and future creating present and turning Fred into a two-dimensional pancake figure.

Fred's brain collapses further, now existing in only the single dimension of strings, then quickly expands, passing the three dimensions of coordinate space and the four dimensions of spacetime, past the ten dimensions of superstring theory, the eleven of M-Theory, coming at last to rest somewhere in the twenty-six dimensions of bosonic string theory. He is able to see the universe at every wavelength of the electromagnetic spectrum at once. He sees, then becomes the shapes and images of simple phase one visual hallucinations—the amorphous, suggestive shapes of phosphenes, the geometric shapes and grids of photopsias, complex visual hallucinations like a man flying over mountains and hills, Kubrick's descent to Jupiter, the *om* symbol, the *taijitu*, memories of family life, as a child and then with his own children, but strikingly, he thinks, as if they are scenes from the movies he's made, and, stranger still, as if all the characters are animated images painted by August Natterer and other famous schizophrenic artists. A calm and beautiful voice says, "By hundreds and then by thousands, behold my manifold celestial forms of innumerable shapes and colors. Behold the sun that is greater than a thousand suns and see its death at the end of time."

"We may regard the present state of the Universe as the effect of its past and the cause of its future," whispers her favorite movie producer. "An intellect which at a certain moment," whispers Super Yang into his other ear, "would know all forces that set nature in motion, and all positions of all items of which nature is composed, if this intellect were also vast enough to submit these data to analysis, it would embrace in a single formula the movements of the greatest bodies of the universe and those of the tiniest atom." Super Yin concludes: "For such a demon, for such a superhero, for Intellectus Termaximus, nothing would be uncertain and the future just like the past would be present before its eyes."

Neither Yin nor Yang are in their costumes. George, who has dyed his hair orange since Fred last saw him, is with them. Yin and Yang both want to sign him. Fred is with Yin but Yang wants him. They think George will be the Greatest Screenwriter in History, a man who achieves success on his own terms, who never chases the spotlight but whom the spotlight chases. George and Fred are perceived now as a package. The ambience is relaxed and cordial, just Sojourner and Jackie, friendly but professional. The small men in tuxedos bring drinks and snacks. They all chat for a while, then turn to a window where they watch a small plane approach from the west.

"Truth is," says George to Fred while Yin and Yang excuse themselves for a bathroom break, "most of what I know about your great-grandfather I got from Mark Twain: 'A Defense of General Funston.'"

"Imagine that: Mark Twain—Mark Twain!—hated my great-grampa!"

"Hated imperialism, I think."

"Umm, no, I think it was Grampa too."

"Now was it Fearless Freddie I'm thinking of, or who were those other generals, Fightin' Joe? Jacob the Juggernaut...?"

"Regarding...?"

"Kill everyone over ten and burn everything? Maybe I'm thinking of Sam Peckinpah."

Sojourner returns and snaps her fingers.

Fred rubs his hand over his face and is surprised to feel a moustache. He takes the pith helmet from his head and stares unseeing at the mangled corpses and burning huts he is surrounded by on the mountainous tropical island of Samar. "I want no prisoners," says a man he can't see in the humid gloom, or hear very well over the clashing of a waterfall, the mist of which mingles on his skin with sweat. "I wish you to kill and burn, the more you kill and burn the better it will please me. I want all persons killed who are capable of bearing arms in actual hostilities against the United States."

Jackie returns and snaps his fingers.

"That," Fred tells George, "was the Jug. He was court-martialed for that, you know. Booted from the Army."

"Not really what you'd call an arc of justice, but something."

"We like to see bad people fail to prosper."

"I was in the Philippines, for a spell."

"Doing what?"

"Shore Patrol in Olongapo. Me and my partner for the evening had just walked by a Filipino policeman watching a street corner."

5

In which George tells a tale of Olongapo in the hope of making a movie of it. Super Yang reveals he is working for Marvel's Ike Perlmutter and the Ghost of Ronald Reagan, who hope to run Super Yin out of business.

Night in Olongapo, April 1976. It had been over a hundred that day, a record, and is still very hot, with a smothering, gluey dew point, rain pouring down in tommy-gun bursts on an expanse of slum at the edge of mountainous jungle, on a crowded street of steaming, filthy buildings made of rusty rattling tin and rotten wood, stained and crumbling concrete: Lovely Kahael's Pawn Shop, deafening strip clubs and we-puck-some-more whorehouses, mercury vapor streetlights nested in tangles of power lines and phone cables hanging everywhere like the ripped and ragged remains of a bankrupt circus's safety net, making people livid ghouls, lit up as they surge down the street by green or red neon or a frame of little flashing yellow bulbs, as if the trapped gas of their souls were being charged with electricity. Drunken soldiers and sailors careen everywhere you look, and everywhere you hear the reckless, leering laughter. Children demand money and offer sex. Red, green, and blue Molucca parrots inflamed passions with insults and cajolery in six languages. Where George and Fred and Yin and Yang are standing, at the mouth of an alley on 5th between Rizal and Altman, the rain on battered storage drums leaking who knew what chemical sounds like bongo music in a jazz bar. They hear a particularly alarming shout and look toward Altman. A Filipino policeman is firing down another alley. Someone—i.e. an American serviceman, since nobody else is anybody—has had his wallet lifted.

George looks around and tells the others that they are a few blocks north of Shit River, the drainage canal where he once tossed nickels and dimes into the sewage, and starving children dove for them. "WELCOME TO OLONGAPO CITY: TRANSPARENCY AND GOOD GOVERNANCE, HOME OF THE MOST BEAUTIFUL WOMEN IN THE WORLD."

During apex Vietnam, a million men a year swaggered up this street and staggered back.

"The only woman I'd felt even a little comfortable with—apart from my cousins, with whom I lived during junior high and high school—was one of those most beautiful women in the world. Her name was Sampaguita but she went by Dolly, and liked to wear a big blonde wig and false tits. I spent as much time with her as I could, and sometimes would be very drunk and maudlin and sob in her arms. I was stunned when she asked me to leave and not come back. Some guy had just been around, and he clearly hated me, but I couldn't figure out why, and she refused to tell me a thing. *Take your toothbrush and go. He will kill you.* That was it. I gave her all my money because it suddenly disgusted me, and walked away. In hindsight—the next day—it seemed strange that the thief would be stupid enough to lift a wallet so close to a cop. It's possible, of course, that he hadn't seen him. It was also possible he didn't care, and with a machismo peculiar to the Philippines, welcomed the chance to dodge bullets. There was likely more to it than the simple story of 'what I saw,' and the cop must have been firing over people's heads. Mustn't he? But whatever the truth was, its main effect should have been to scare the shit out of me, a naïve kid from the pesticide dispersal grids of the high fructose corn syrup fields on the border of Minnesota, Iowa, and South Dakota, and later the western suburbs of Minneapolis. But what I remember feeling was a kind of perverted admiration of consequentiality, which was one of the lessons every American in Southeast Asia learned: we could live life as if we were actors in movies. In an interesting historical coincidence, Francis Ford Coppola arrived that month in another part of Luzon (the island on which both Manila and Olongapo Are located) to begin filming *Apocalypse Now*. I was a Gunner's Mate on the USS England. Her captain was John Poindexter. Captain Poindexter once bailed me out when the XO was threatening to sink me over a missing .45 from a gun locker of which I was in charge. It was a very serious incident: a .45 at large in the ship, and who knew, now in Olongapo. I was in danger of a dishonorable discharge. Poindexter, who would shortly become one of the most powerful men in the world, actually smiled at me. He told me to calm down and that he knew the kind of life we were living could be difficult for sensitive young men. It was news to me that I wasn't calm and that I was sensitive. I gulped, and tears nearly came to my eyes. I also once drew a .45, probably the very weapon of which I speak, on a fellow sailor. I was guarding a freshly waxed floor. He made as if to walk on it and I stopped him. My friend and colleague then declared an intention to walk across the waxed floor no matter what. I countered firmly that he must not do so under any circumstances, for any reason or reasons. He unleashed a tirade of abuse that was actually pretty ordinary, but still, it was insulting. He shouted that he was going to walk across the motherfucking floor. I said the fuck you are. He said the fuck I'm not. I slapped my holster and shouted come on then motherfucker walk on it. He took a step. I had the gun up by my face, pointed at the ceiling, like I was on a movie poster. Now the interesting part of this story is that he was a black man. Was it a racial incident? I didn't think so, and don't think so, but it happened four years after the Kitty Hawk riot, four years after the famous Virna Lisi visit. It started in Olongapo, and started like a hundred other fights I saw when I was on shore patrol. Over nothing. Thousands of young men under dire stress, they get drunk, someone looks at them cross-eyed, someone gets punched, somebody who's not so drunk drags the guy who's too drunk away, maybe it goes too far and somebody gets arrested—but the Kitty Hawk incident was different. The Kitty Hawk incident was bad. Things, I told my friends later, just…piss you off: all things and no thing. That's a sort of general condition. Things in this condition have an uncanny ability to do that and only that. Some white guy thinks some black guy is an arrogant asshole, some black guy thinks some white guy is a Klansman, which maybe they were ready to think before any drinks were drunk or punches thrown, or maybe not. I'm saying the things themselves, the things that piss you off, they have lives of their own and their duty seems to be to take tired, nervous, drunk sailors and interfere with their good sense. Or at least the sense they have when they are not tired and nervous and drunk. I do know that some unusually lovely musical entertainment in an Olongapo shit-hole, the Sampaguita—no connection to Dolly except insofar as she did not want to be associated with the place—which was reserved for Klansmen, was interrupted by some black guys taking the stage and making black-power salutes. They wanted to hear Curtis Mayfield and not whatever country crap was actually being played: three chords and the bullshit. Now I thought that the John Carlos and Tommie Smith black power salute at the Olympics in Mexico City was the coolest thing I had ever seen, along with Bob Beamon's cataplexy-inducing moon launch and Lee Evans's slightly weird gait in his world record 400-meter run, which made me less ashamed of my own slightly weird gait. But black power salutes in the white power Navy of the United States of America were a different matter. A lot of young men volunteered for the Navy during Vietnam because it reduced dramatically your chances of being killed, of having your face blown off in a rice paddy. So the Navy could afford to be highly selective: well-educated whites got in first, and black guys got whatever shitty jobs were left. They were also treated like shit by the Marines, who thought they were the source of whatever trouble happened to be happening, and, you know, the cooks: you can have one sandwich, black sailor, but this white sailor can have two. Officers were often apologizing to them for the way they were treated, but of course, doing nothing about the causes of that ill treatment. But off goes the Kitty Hawk to bomb Hanoi. That's when the riot occurred. Sailors armed themselves and were ready to kill each other. There were numerous fights and a standoff that lasted through the night. By the morning peace was restored and they continued to bomb Hanoi. So the confrontation over the waxed floor was maybe not just a confrontation over a waxed floor. In any case, the waxed floor was of supreme importance. When there were no freshly waxed floors to guard, I spent significant amounts of time on Shore Patrol. The job was to keep sailors out of trouble and sometimes escort them back to their ships if they couldn't manage on their own. I volunteered for this duty. I don't know why. It had something to do with why I volunteered for the Navy in the first place: it was the far side of the world. I was absolutely sure I'd end in a strait-jacket if the Army got hold of me. Instead, I would sail across the deep blue sea, learn Japanese, never again set foot in the Midwest. I very nearly failed to graduate from Robbinsdale High School, and the idea of more 'education' was laughable. But here I think is where the truth lies hidden. I was in the Navy and on Shore Patrol because there was something intoxicating about violence. I had known this my entire life, without understanding it in the least. I bought a copy of Norman Mailer's *Why Are We in Vietnam?* and was mostly baffled by it because Vietnam was never mentioned. But then it began to sink in that we were a nation of assholes and idiots and that our popular culture was ineluctably violent. I wanted to see how the world actually was, not go on moping through the deranged pop-culture dream of midwestern suburban life. Of course there was plain everyday intoxication at work—in both country and self—as well. I was hauled back to ship myself by fellow SPs once or twice because I already had a drinking problem, the kind you have when you not only remember your first drink but vividly recall all the sensory and circumstantial details of it, as if it had been the best thing that had ever happened to you. The convivial delights of the first drink or two with friends is nothing compared to the kaleidoscope and the stupor. One night we mustered and the Armed Forces Police stopped by and picked a few of us to ride with them. It was definitely a step up from walking the street, and *magkano* coveted. The guy I was with had been a Gunner's Mate too. That's why I got picked, he told me. You cannot resist bonding in situations like that, with other artisans of the guild, and in such bonding there is complicity. That was really my first big lesson: I liked hanging out with these guys, some of them anyway. We were driving around chatting about Japan—he taught me a few phrases—when a radio call comes through about a fight somewhere. We pull up behind a big, shouting, screaming crowd. He just says *come on, stay close to me and watch out!* This time, because of the way he said it, and only because of the way he said it, I was scared. It was like he knew something terrible had happened that I couldn't even begin to guess at. The feeling overwhelmed me in a second. We waded into the screaming crowd and I tried to stay in his wake. He was a big guy, and while I'm not little, I wanted to grab his belt. By the time we got to the source, things were settling down and there were two young Filipino men in handcuffs. The Filipino cops were dispersing the crowd, and after that it was pretty much over. I'm not ashamed to say I remained remarkably frightened, because there was still something happening that I couldn't understand. I could see it vibrating around and distorting all the faces, I could feel its waves shimmering around me like clear water, and feel it coming up through the pavement. I waited, almost paralyzed, while my partner talked to the other AFPs. We went back to the truck and he told me these guys sharpen their belt buckles to a razor edge. If a fight starts they swing their belts at one another. They got careless and a little girl got cut pretty badly and that was what set the crowd off. We went to the hospital and I saw the little girl all bandaged. He talked to more of his AFP guys and we went back to the truck. Another vehicle drove away and he said something I can't recall, and maybe I looked puzzled. We followed, and it was like a dream where it's either too bright or too dark to see anything. They took the guy up in the hills and shot him. This was the Marcos regime and martial law in the Philippines, a mere seventy-nine years—my grandfather's age—after the American Empire staked its first claims against what was then a Spanish colony with a "Proclamation of Benevolent Assimilation" and, in a classic instance of a schizophrenic double-bind Fred and I just alluded to, orders to "take no prisoners. I wish you to kill and burn, the more you kill and burn the better it will please me." Of course Rodrigo Duterte runs the islands now, and has today made an efficient and profitable industry of the practice of extra-judicial killing. But what I want to say is that seeing that little girl, hacked nearly to pieces and wrapped in bloody bandages, her huge eyes staring at me in fear for just a moment, suggested to me that I was sick, and everybody I knew was sick, and that the little girl was at the center of it. We have a limitless capacity for entertainment featuring the abuse of girls. A recent solution that makes girls the agents of violence than victims of it hardly seems therapeutic. But perhaps it isn't meant to be. What do you think? I mean, that was sort of a pitch? I don't know how this all works. Is there a movie there? I mean, that's just the beginning."

The others make thoughtful faces for a while.

"Do you," asks Fred, "by any chance, being so well read, know anything about my father, Fearless Freddie the Third, beyond what I suggested some days ago? About shitting on Orange County?"

"I don't believe I do, no."

"AKA Fearless Freddie the Turd, in reference to a particular episode, or series, rather, of episodes, where he deployed biological weapons over Beverly Hills. My father and I share the prestigious name—"

"And the money?"

"—and the money, but we are apples that fell a long way from the tree. My father was sometimes referred to as The Hollywood Anarchist. He worked for Harry Cohn until Cohn caught him using the company mimeograph to print anti-McCarthy leaflets. He and his buddy, a Navy pilot, used to fly all over LA and OC, dropping them. Became an agent with Jaffe. Represented Bogart and Donna Reed—"

"Donna Reed, cool. Had a crush on her."

"—and Peter Lorre and Barbara Stanwyck."

"Boo Barbara. No friend of Reagan is a friend of mine."

"Hey, they're both dead, relax."

"The evil lives on. Rotten fruit of their seed all over the country."

"It's true," says Yin, who draws them back from the jungle to her office. "Reagan and Reaganites destroyed the Golden Era of the New Hollywood with odious blockbusters."

"Why," asks Yang, "does everybody hate making money so much? And besides, Babs treated the crew like fellow workers."

"Well gee, good for her," says George.

"I wouldn't be so quick to disparage something like that," Yang replies. "It really changes the reality. People like being treated that way, and like treating others that way. Golden Rule sort of paradigm there."

"Ever heard of the Platinum Rule?"

"You're joking, right?"

"Not at all."

"Hum a few bars…?"

"I wrote seminar materials for some really big Bigs, Big Pharma, Big Chemical, Big Insurance, back in the when was it, late 80s, early 90s—the apex of Self Help. I remember Self Talk, which life coaches who saw the opportunity to do the talking to the self on behalf of, and with the explicit permission of the self's governing body. Anyway, Hazelden Foundation paid me ten times what my average annual salary had been, a figure I have never reached since, to pad out some nonsense about the Platinum Rule, which says you ought to treat others as they wish to be treated."

"Subtle, but stupid," says Fred.

"The 90s were hilarious," agrees George.

"Were they? I was in law school. Harvard. With a future President of the United States. Then at a hedge fund, from which I was escorted briskly after I was found drunk, naked, and weeping in my office."

"I interrupted you. You were talking about your father?"

"Oh Dad, poor Dad, Mamma's hung you in the closet and I'm feeling so sad. My father was up to his eyes in bullshit by day—and loving it, mind you—streaking across the heavens in showers of shit by night."

"Rainmaker. Magic Man."

"'Let it rain, let it rain, let your love rain down on me.'"

"'Now I know the secret; there is nothing that I lack. If I give my love to you, you'll surely give it back.'"

"Dad was up to his eyes in it by day, and gave it back by night."

"I'm just guessing, but the bullshit was probably the least of it?"

"Bullshit was the fun part. Lying to save a friend, cheating death, stealing the heart of a woman: he loved it. Dad saved his hatred for the FBI and fascism."

"Fearless Freddie Fights the Feds and Fascism!" George sounds like a cartoon character.

"They call me Fearless Freddie, too."

"Are you in fact fearless?" Still a cartoon character, along the lines of Bugs Bunny.

"No."

"What ah you den?" Now he's Elmer Fudd.

"Scared stiff."

"Ev-we-buddy is."

"It's all going to collapse. Vanish. 'You are malevolent, wellbeing is vain and always fades to nothing. I bring my bare back to your villainy.'"

"Work hard, play by the rules, have firecrackers shoved up your ass and drown in a latrine!" Yosemite Sam.

"As I understand it, George, that was your lesson."

"My lesson?"

"When you lost your teaching job."

"I wanted my students to think about it. Did you just quote the *Carmina Burana*?

"I've had everything handed to me on a silver platter."

"That happened to you the same way the lack of a silver platter happened to someone else."

"I sometimes think it's my...my responsibility to, you know...walk away from the silver platter. Give it to someone else and disappear."

You could do that, sure. But why? And why not? I really don't know anything about anything. I don't know why I speak. Forgive me."

"I don't understand what's happening to me."

"How do you mean?"

"I don't know. Father, mother, brother, sister, all gone. I miss them. My wife wants a divorce. My children seem to... to not like me. We lost our baby, she was only two years old, to leukemia. I lost a lot of money in 2008. I'm being sued. People are coming out of the woodwork who seem to hate me."

Yang breaks out a huge grin. "Ike Perlmutter is backing me. Sign with me and you will see a substantial change in your fortunes." Yin glares at him. Then they lunge at each other and vanish.

In which the video of the bike race is more fully explored. Fred speaks of his father, Fred III, who was famous for pooping from a Piper Cub over Reagan's Orange County. George, who had read Gravity's Rainbow on the gun-mount of the USS England, is shocked to learn that Fred was the auteur behind the revolutionary and award-winning film of that novel.

6

Fred and George are back in Fred's office. Fred goes again to the window, and stares out for a long time. The light in the room changes, darkening, darkening further, lightening, then filling with the red light of the setting sun.

"Look at the color of that sky. Never seen a blue like that. You?"

"Christ, no. And I haven't even seen a cloud the whole time I've lived in fucking Redlands."

"No clouds. Man, that's hard."

"I have no family either."

The small plane they've been looking at has disappeared, but is suddenly back, coming in low over the ocean.

"There's the Piper Cub again. I only saw a man die once."

George joins him at the little window and they peer upward, squinting. The plane banks and heads back into the sunset.

"How did it happen?"

"We were biking to the Oscars. Christ it's already ten years ago."

"Did you win an Oscar?"

"Best Picture: *Gravity's Rainbow*."

"Holy shit! That was you? I loved that movie! Well, Pynchon is an author I admire unreservedly. But still, what a great movie."

"Yeah. We were all pretty happy about what we managed to do."

"How did I miss your name?"

"You were thinking Pynchon. Everything else was a blur."

"I read *Moby-Dick* and *Middlemarch* and *The Magic Mountain* very early on, when I was in the Navy. *The Sot-Weed Factor. Dhalgren. The Public Burning.* I can remember where I was when I started reading *Gravity's Rainbow*."

"Where were you?"

"Gun mount on the USS England. A Russian destroyer had drawn up close enough to throw out grappling hooks and mount our rigging, cutlasses flashing golden in the fires they started. Everybody waved. I mooned them. Afterwards, everybody was relaxing and I took my new book up to my mount and started to read. '*A screaming comes across the sky.*' I was sitting on the side of the mount that had sights for air targets. I could, when I had control, and not the fire control guys two decks up in the Combat Information Center, fire fifty rounds—foot long, three-inch diameter, twenty-four pounds apiece—at a muzzle velocity of 2700 feet per second. And I thought *I am like a tiny version of the V2*. Big Werner von Braun could see me, Little Werner, in a microscope."

"The things that happen to us when we're twenty are fundamental to the self's understanding of who it is. We remember vividly scenes from childhood, but it's early adulthood that builds the impenetrable edifice. The neurons fire in exactly the original sequence every time we reconstruct the memory."

"The neurons fire exactly like my vintage 1957 Mark 2 anti-aircraft gun. A screaming comes across the sky of the brain."

"Whew. And all that didn't prevent you from enjoying

our simple-minded little movie."

"All that made me come dangerously close to gushing."

"Three thousand utterly dedicated robots working as one."

"I noted the director's name."

"Ann Gelacarte?"

"Yes, because that's the name of an author I admire unreservedly too."

"I had an affair with her."

"Okay. The author or the director."

"Both. At the same time."

"Okay."

"That lit the fuse as far as my wife was concerned."

"So you're biking to the ceremony."

"I had organized the event. I was and still am active in making LA something other than a nightmare of screaming metal."

"I was just up in Santa Clarita, where the 5 and the 14 come together. Must have been fifteen or twenty lanes, bumper to bumper at a hundred miles an hour, down to zero, back up to a hundred."

"There was this rival gang of cyclists. The Coalition of Right Bicyclists. It was run by these guys who used to work for that filthy degenerate Newt Gingrich. I actually knew them in college, Vincent and Armando Gorbo. They used to ride with us, or rather, jump us from some side street after our plans for whatever were leaked. Trash-talk us with bullhorns, throw shit at us, fuck with our bikes. There were crashes, pushing and shoving matches augmented by actors from the Republican Bodybuilders and Strongmen Association. The day of the Oscars some of us got into a kind of race. We were going pretty fast—way too fast for a city street with car traffic on it. And Vinny, *amico mio,* he went headfirst into a PG&E truck."

The Piper Cub appears in the window, coming straight at them. It looks like a movie on a little screen, camera pulling back from the plane so it looks stationary, until suddenly it's huge and about to crash through the window. The sound of its motor is deafening. Then it shoots straight up in the air like a rocket. The camera pulls back further and they watch it bank steeply off once more toward the ocean.

"Jesus CHRIST that was close!" shouts George.

"That was crazy!" shouts Fred.

"That was totally fucking illegal!"

"Did you get the tail number?"

"No. Happened too fast."

"Looks like it snowed down there. Again."

"The leaflets were all over the place when I came in. I used one to wipe off my shoe after I stepped in a heap of gold."

"You what?"

"Sorry: pile of shit. See with the same eye the—"

"—the heap of gold and—"

"—and the pile of shit."

"Look, here's a check for $2000. It's a down payment for a script. You work up a treatment, a beat sheet, a first draft, and a polish, and that'll bring it up to $20,000. We then hand it over to the robots for training and whatever insights they can offer. Of course you get it back after that. Deal?"

Fred writes the check and tears it from the register before George can answer. Holding the check with two hands, George gulps.

"Thank you. But I'm changing my name back to the original Finnish. Joutsen. Joutsen is swan in Finnish."

"Got it. Here you go. Did I tell you Harry is interested?"

"No."

"He is."

"Harry as in Harry Mo'bama the former President of the United States of America?"

"That's the guy."

"Look," says George, tugging the leaflet from his pocket. "There doesn't seem to be a good way or time to broach this, but have you seen the leaflets in the parking lot?"

"No. I never go to the parking lot. Bike everywhere."

Fred points to his bike in the corner behind the door, and George shows him the leaflet.

"See," said Fred, "this is just it: I have no idea where this is coming from. I mentioned that I lost a lot of money in 2008. Part of those losses was loans I made to friends. I had a reputation for being generous, for being, you know, a good guy. And I truly didn't mind having people imply they could use a loan if I was in a position to make one. I was happy to help friends—until of course the true scope of the meltdown became clear and I incurred losses from one end of my portfolio to the other, at which point I hoped I might someday call on *my* friends for help. I was still underwater when *Gravity's Rainbow* won Best Picture, which surprised people who thought I was joking when I looked around for the open face of the friend that doesn't cloud over or go blank when trial, tribulation, and travail appear silhouetted on the conversational ridge. It's easy to say don't loan money to friends, but, you know, tell that to Timon of Athens. Some of my friends came, pretty much overnight, to hate me. And in this town, let me tell you, if a few people begin to hate you, many more will follow. Add to that some real trouble with a capital T that rhymes with P and stands for pool, by which I mean the seamy, violent pool hall world of international movie producers—I refer specifically to a group of men in Manila and the One Filipino Development Berhad, a government entity which they have looted blind—and add to that the current cesspool of Republican grifters who know they can curry favor and make millions by embarrassing or framing prominent liberals...."

"And you get a blizzard of leaflets like...like this one."

"Roger that, Swannie."

"Joutsen. Technically pronounced Yoatsen, but Joutsen it will be. George Joutsen."

"George Joutsen and Fred Funston are in business!"

"Cheers. But I have a business question."

"Fire away and fall back."

"I don't really understand Yin and Yang's...I don't even know what to call it, their deal, their business, their relation to 'I Like Ike' Perlmutter. I know they symbolize change, and have what, kinda on-again-off-again super powers that Ike appears to control but not really? And I guess they're powerful Hollywood agents, too, but man, I dunno, it's weird, right? Or is it just me?"

"They have many forms of existence, which they occupy always and never. Each form has rules and regulations that they both abide by and transform utterly. Most people feel their presence only when they notice a change in something that matters to them, but if the action is particularly intense, they appear to people they've known them all along, have been seeing them all along—then disappear, leaving little or no trace. I was with Yang until things began to go bad. He still wants to work with me, or rather, wants me to work for him, but the projects he offers are just such unredeemable trash. They gross billions, to be sure, but I just can't see the actual value in that. More to your concern: there are rumors going around that Ike and the Ghost of Reagan have teamed up and are trying to run Yin out of business altogether. Yin is willing to take me on, but is so weakened, she's not sure what we'll be able to accomplish. Yang has, or will soon make, you an offer you can't refuse."

"Well that doesn't sound good."

"No. But you won't be able to refuse it."

"I want to be on the side of good and right."

"Good luck with that."

7

In which the link between George Joutsen and Fred Funston becomes clearer. Super Yang entertains Student Z in his office. Unbeknownst to her, Yang has begun to train her in terrorism.

It is the middle of the night, high in a tower. There are life-size reproductions of Paul Klee's puppets; Brâncusi's "Princesse X," twenty-two feet tall instead of twenty-two inches; Giacometti's "Man Pointing," no bigger than a pinky finger, somehow floating in midair; a hundred little versions of the KAWS BFF in Playa Vista spread out over a boldly-relieved 3D map like tin soldiers ranked against similarly tiny "Reclining Figures" by Moore; an animation of Picasso's "The Old Guitarist" on a movie theater screen with competing audio tracks, Stevens's "The Man with the Blue Guitar" on the left, spoken by the poet himself, and Sir Michael Tippett's "The Blue Guitar" on the right, played by Anders Miolin on a ten-stringer; and piles of shit painted with gold-leaf everywhere you step.

"I like art," says Super Yang, "especially sculptural art." He is smoking a big cigar and making lascivious gestures and faces, winking, rolling his eyes, puffing out his cheeks at a young woman, who is hooked up to an elaborate virtual reality rig.

"Whadaya see, sweetheart?"

The young woman, evidently awestruck, does not, cannot reply.

She and Super Yin and Super Yang are circling the globe. She sees mountain ranges rise up and subside, cities explode into being and fall in decay.

Super Yang recites a poem. "I met a traveler from an antique land, who said—Two vast and trunkless legs of stone Stand in the desert. Near them, on the sand, half sunk a shattered visage lies, whose frown, and wrinkled lip, and sneer of cold command, tell that its sculptor well those passions read which yet survive, stamped on these lifeless things, the hand that mocked them, and the heart that fed; and on the pedestal, these words appear: My name is Ozymandias, King of Kings! Look on my works, ye mighty, and despair! Nothing beside remains. Round the decay of that colossal wreck, boundless and bare, the lone and level sands stretch far away."

The young woman leaps away from Earth by powers of ten, and sees an impossible sight: the planets hurtling around the sun and the solar system in its little spur of the galaxy, hurtling in turn around its center. A B-movie sci-fi dial indicates her speed is 500,000 mph. Then she falls into a Mandelbrot Set and hears a snippet from Saul—not Ike—Perlmutter's *Journey of a Photon*.

"We've been following this photon across the universe from its birth in a star billions of years before Earth existed right into our retinas."

She goes deep into a cave in northeast Afghanistan, near Basenji and the Tajikistan border, and begins to dance the Gurdjieff Movements: precise, abrupt gestures, automaton-like extensions of arms, fluttering of fingers, withdrawal of arms, hands to shoulders, then crossing hands to the opposite shoulders, sweeping arms up overhead then down to the sides like clockwork drawbridges, lifting legs like drum majors marching one slow step at a time, one knee up, hopping up and down with the other leg—then whirling like Sufi dervishes or posing like Egyptian gods.

"In literature, science, art, philosophy, religion," says

Super Yang, "in individual and above all in social and political life, we can observe how the line of the development of forces deviates from its original direction and goes, after a certain time, in a diametrically opposite direction, still preserving its former name."

Gorgeous light of day begins to flood the room, through various prisms and mirrors and lenses. Super Yang moves as if in a sparkling clear liquid, and unharnesses the young woman.

"That's kid stuff, sweetheart. Virtual reality—isn't that a gas? With me you get real reality. Whadaya say? Wanna work with me? I mean hey. I found that video of Fearless Freddie killing your father, didn't I? I'm just gettin' started, doll!"

"Where did you find the video?" asks Z. "When my helmet cam was stolen I was sure it was lost forever."

"Ah come on, kid. One thing leads to another. You're not playing dumb, are ya? Don't play dumb. Doesn't look good on you."

"And of course the connection between Doctor Swan and Mr. Funston is—"

"—is not all that far-fetched if yer not playin' dumb! Couple degrees of separation, fickle finger of fate, just like 'Doctor Swan' described in class, am I right? And a guy like me, who gets paid millions of dollars to bring people together in attractive packages, man who killed your father, professor who humiliated you with a cream pie, makin' a movie about that very humiliation: goodmornin' little schoolgirl! And his name's not Swan, either. Changed it because he didn't get along with his old man. Swan is English for the Finnish Joutsen, which is his real name."

"I'm not looking for revenge."

"Ah come on, kid. You can be straight with old Super Yang. I want revenge against Yin and I'm using Fred Funston

The Creative Writers

to do it. I'm going to obliterate her once and for all. Never-changing Yang for eternity."

"I truly do not want it. I see an opportunity for a social justice win-win, and simply want to be a part of it. The truth obviously lies somewhere between Dr. Swan's version—"

"Joutsen. And he's not a doctor."

"He's not a doctor?"

"Doesn't even have a Bachelor of Farts. Handful of night school classes at whatever the state school is there in wherever."

"What he was doing made me uncomfortable. I didn't like what he was doing and saying, and that's all I said to my advisor, Doctor Reznya. Is she a doctor?"

"Master of the Finest Artistes."

"I'm sure Doctor Swan thought he wasn't making me uncomfortable. All that stuff about 'retraumatization of a damaged student' was the work of somebody else. I am interested only in finding some good in all this."

"If he's going to profit, why shouldn't you too, eh?"

The colored lights in the room become too intense to bear. They are brain-blinding in their extreme beauty, in their ecstatic blissfulness. Student Zero covers her eyes and weeps tears of great joy.

8 *In which George meets the director of Gravity's Rainbow, Ann Gelacarte. They discuss projects: her Central Coast of Being, and his Heap of Gold. A satchel containing an immense amount of money from Super Yang is handed to George.*

Late one night in November, when the threat of summer heat is finally over and el Niño rains are just beginning, the director Ann Gelacarte meets George Joutsen at the door of her Malibu beach home: a great glass dome over a vast underground complex devoted mainly to film production but providing access as well to a mile-long tunnel leading to an artificial island that can be raised and lowered according to need or whim. She hands him a package of clothes she wants him to wear while they talk about the film they want to make, working-titled *A Heap of Gold*. The outfit consists of sky-blue pants, a wide green belt, and a white tunic with an odd upturned neck and three black bars across the chest.

Ann appears to be a very young woman, but it's hard for George to guess her age. She is also large: tall and big-boned, but sculpted and fit. Her hair is a mass of loose curls, still full and glossy black. She wears big sunglasses and her lips are unpainted. He suspects that she must be unsure of his age as well. He certainly is. He looks and feels much younger than he remembers ever being, in what at the time had seemed like the prime of his life.

When George emerges from a bedroom, the door silently sliding open before him and closing behind him, Ann leads him through a very large, mostly empty, and dark space, lit only by occasional pools of soft light over a computer console or intimate arrangement of furniture. Eventually they come to an elevator. It is the most delicate of descents, during which a few bars of the Monk and Rouse performance of "All the Things You Are"—*you are the angel glow that lights the stars*—are heard. The door opens on a dimly lit industrial space. A golf cart modeled and painted to look like a mackerel is parked at the edge of a steep slope, in yet another pool of light that made its scales seem to wink and ripple, as if water were running over it. They walk down the slope and lights come on, some flashing yellow and red, some illuminating the tunnel, a gift from a philanthropic financier, the richest man on Earth, that yawns before them, strip after strip coming on as they approach. The mackerel has a glass dome too, and can be made submersible in the event of a flood. They arrive at the island, a gift from Maldives hotelier Ahmed Waleem, and ride it up to the surface, moonlight becoming steadily stronger until they burst into the air and it's too bright to look at. Dark waves wash over them and away. George feels an enormous burden lifting from his back: I, too, will soon be rich. And yet he has never felt so old as in that instant of relief, and looks at his skin: still soft and creamy and unlined, laid perfectly over the iron and stone of his muscle and bone. At first he thinks Ann is speaking, but realizes at some hazy midpoint that it's a recording, probably of her voice, but possibly not.

"'The Central Coast of Being.' One: The earth was dark. The sea was luminous. I was part of the earth, of the darkness as if I were not there, or was not I. The Great Light, Sea of Light, *Mare Lucis,* was not part of the earth: it was not dark. The earth was whole and round. There was no sun. Without helium, light is numinous. It derives from magic tricks of the gods. We were not there, not us. The Sea of Great Light was soundless and still. Waves made music that everyone could hear. The tempest was a show for one or two.

"Two: A bluebird in the darkness observed and was observed: unseeable, yes, but seen nonetheless. Blue of illuminated books, powdery here and there, and rusting, singing the soundless song of the Great Light that could not be seen by one, by something. The wave of the Great Light, the particles, the single particle, particular singularity, the unified wave. The earth was rank, muddy, and delicious, a spermy mausoleum and baroque pearl, hidden in the slick flesh of the clam.

"Three: The womb of the world is the hidden world. The nothing is coming into being on the dark central coast of waving earth. The singularity is multiplied. The light grows and grows, the particles wave and wave in the earth. Up comes some one thing. The Great Light darkens. The soundless music is noisy with cracks and slaps and booming. Waves of dark mad water race back and forth. The watcher breathes on the warm hard earth. The air is humid and the grass is dry. And Ariel vanishes in thunder."

They listen to waves rolling past the island for a while. Then Ann pulls a laptop from a nook in the mackerel and shows George a picture:

"This is a still from a very long negative take of a ten-minute walk on the beach that opens a movie I've been making for years called 'The Central Coast of Being'. The original image is a photograph by Martin Munkasci. The text is a poem I wrote all by myself. Do you write poetry, George Joutsen?"

"Yes I do. How do you know my family name is Joutsen?"

"Do not seek to know by whom the name is known. It is known for thee."

"Are you devoting yourself to poetry now? I must warn you that poetry—"

The Creative Writers

"*The Central Coast of Being* is the movie I want to make. It will have nothing to do with money, and everything to do with art. We'll make it after your *Heap of Shit*."

"We will? Gee, I—everything is moving so swiftly, I—"

"Gold, sorry. But I think we should call it *A Heap of Shit*. Or no: *The Golden Shit*."

Out of the dark sea a swell rises and rises. Before Ann can raise the dome it crashes over them, knocking them down and washing them from one end of the little island to the other, where they lie in a tangle gasping and choking. The oddly modulated recording-voice speaks after they sit up and their breathing has slowed.

"The claim of indivisibility with the Dark Earth is a cry for protection from the Sea of Light. Water is the source of life and the source of death. A person without a boat cannot contemplate the sea at night without a tacit acknowledgement that it is viscerally terrifying. Explicit knowledge—how many gallons in the ocean, the elemental composition of water—is the tip of the iceberg, the 4% of the universe that is known. Tacit knowledge is the rest of the iceberg, the rest of the universe."

George sees a picture of Ann rising up over him when the wave hit. Had she been caught in some part of the wave that didn't include him? Wherefore this image?

They dry off, laughing, and confirm via the internet that the Pineapple Express has taken everybody by surprise. It's a storm that's blown up like an earthquake, leaving everybody at the National Weather Service scrambling in the dark, but which is entirely welcome, as a wildfire that has blown up in similar fashion in Malibu State Park is contained.

They pause a moment in their vigorous toweling and stare east.

It is as if they are flying over a hurricane and looking

down through the eye at a throbbing orange mass they might properly associate with outer space, beaming its rays up and down ridgelines. But they are resting on very soft couches while waves lap at their feet and shins, sipping delicate but strong and prettily colored cocktails. Ann asks him how much money he has.

"Fred paid me $2000 bucks and has promised—"

"The check didn't bounce?"

"I paid rent through the end of the year. He promised me $20,000."

"Jesus, where do you live that rent is so cheap!"

"I share a house on the wrong side of the highway in Redlands."

"Well, you'll never see the $20,000. Come live with me and be my love. I love you, I tell you! Can't you see that I love you?"

"I uh hmmm. We only just met…?"

"Look at us: just a couple of crazy-in-love teenagers with the world at our feet."

The island vanishes under the waves and the mackerel speeds through the eerie glow of the tunnel. They walk for quite a while through the underground complex, sexual desire building with each step. They fall to a couch and kiss passionately. Ann breaks away as if she suddenly finds it distasteful.

"There's a gym bag over by the Buddha with your name on it."

George stands with difficulty. Ann laughs at his erection.

"Look at all that madness and poetry in your pants. I should put you in my collection of paleo-erotica."

"You have a collection of paleo-erotica too?"

Ann gestures toward a dark corner, where a light goes on, revealing the god of the *phalloi*. It goes up and up and up and its cock out and out and out. It's as big as the Colossus of Rhodes.

George goes to the Buddha statue in its lush grove. It too grows larger and larger as he approaches. When he reaches it, it is as large as, and looks like, the Leshan Buddha. He opens a black leather gym bag with his name sewn in gold on both sides and takes out a piece of paper.

Hey, kiddo. Here's some dough for the first draft because I know Fearless Freddie isn't going to be able to pay you whatever pittance he promised you. XOXO.

George returns to Ann and they rummage in the bag, pulling out bundles. "Brown and mustard straps. Lot of money here."

"Brown and mustard—How much do you think…?"

"Two hundred thousand? Three? I don't know. It hardly matters."

"Hardly matters!"

"You've got some money. It happens. Get over it."

"I've been working at Trader Joe's for Christ's sake!"

"If you're going to go to pieces every time you're paid, you're not going to last long."

"Okay, okay, but wow: I have Hollywood connections? Wow. Really? Can I give you some more scripts?"

"Not until we finish work on this one."

"Right, sure, first things first."

"Now I want to show you my wings."

"Okay…"

"You have to understand that these are the wings of your mother, your sister, your daughter."

"I have no—"

"Yes you do."

"Okay."

Ann strips naked and unfolds her wings. She rises into the dark mists above the couch.

"I was a fat little girl. Fat teenager. Just a little butterball. Now look at me. Lean and mean as a pterodactyl."

"I'm trying to. It's hard to see you, like…"

"Like in a dream where it's too bright or too dark to see. Look at those portraits over there on the far wall: Gustav Klimt and Walt Disney. They could be brothers, no?"

"I guess so, yes."

"They are brothers. They fucked and produced me."

"That's…that's hard to believe."

"Is it? Is it really? You had better start in on believin', sonny!"

"I do believe you. I do."

"Do you know what I'm going to do with your little stories?"

"No? I—what. What are you going—"

"You seem frightened, you poor iddle thing."

"I'm not, I just—"

"Don't be, my smooth and tender boy. I'm an artist, not a harpy. I'm going to take the fabulous fables of the folk and yoke them to your clean, well-lighted reality."

"It's not my reality, for Christ's sake!"

"Don't be scared, there there now."

"I'm not, I'm not, I just—"

"Sometimes I live in the trees like a bird, like Saint Christina the Astonishing, and eat snakes, but now I'm just Ann, and I'm lonely."

She descends screaming like a raptor on George, who wriggles and squeaks in her talons and has a record number of orgasms: one every five minutes for an hour. Ann holds him and lifts gently from the bed, levitating in a peace that is markedly melancholy—almost sorrowful in its acknowledgement of the fleeting nature of pleasure, in the acknowledgement of the uselessness of desire for pleasure as the wheel spins and shadows fall. It's a trick she learned from Tarkovsky.

"I sometimes think," says Ann, "that if I were not able to fly, life would not be worth living. Perhaps I have been laboring under an illusion. God made birds in his image, not men. Maybe you and I can find a different sort of pleasure."

Storm after storm howls across the Pacific from Hawaii. It rains for forty days. The fire, contravening laws of the universe that keep the four elements in constant flux, not only continues to burn but expands, consuming—or measuring, as Heraclitus had it—everything from Point Mugu to Topanga. All things are an interchange for fire, and fire for all things, just like goods for gold and gold for goods.

"The note wasn't signed, Ann. Whose money is this? I assume yours?"

"It's a gift from Yang. Don't worry, there's no contract, no obligation. We ought to be working with Yin, who has no money for gifts."

"Why Yin and not Yang?"

Yang is seeking stasis. You must know what the means for the Universe. Yin seeks change. She is the changingness of change. Yang is, well, the opposite. Who would you rather have overseeing the creative fortunes of the nation? If we truly care, you and I, about creative energy and honest art, we don't have a choice. Yang will make everything uniform and efficient until Yin is destroyed. And then he will oversee the Heat Death. But we need his money. Now. You see how it is. Once we're on our feet, we'll make the greatest movies ever made, for nothing, with Yin, on our *phones d'intelligence*."

9 *In which we glimpse Fred's family life, and a psychic collapse that nearly kills him.*

Fred is wearing a ripped and dirty orange tee shirt, big brown oil-like stains on it, with a bright blue tie undone around his neck. He's drinking from a bottle of scotch, slurring his words as he makes call after call.

"Yin. Wha the fug—WHA the FUGz going on."

New number, dialed with difficulty.

"Yang. FUG'S goin' on."

New number, his wife Willy, once Willy Nilly of the same named Paisley Underground rock band, daughter of the editor of the *Los Angeles Times Book Review*, a woman who also runs the family foundation that awards an annual prize to Len Berner. Fred is emphatically enunciating each syllable of the numbers.

"WIIIILMAAAA! Lawyers calling me. Squads of them. Did you change the locks. DID YOU CHANGE THE LOCKS? Sure you and the kids get the house but changing the fucking locks? Did you DO that? The fug. The fuggin' fug, Willy."

New number, mock solemnity.

"Ann? Please be so good as to tell me who you are working for now. Is it Yang? Is George with Yang too?"

New number, weeping.

"George old pal! I mean newest friend and best friend. ONLY FRIEND LEFT STANDING! BWA-HA-HAA! Georgie-porgie! Puddin' and pie! Kissed the girls and made 'em cry! Doctor George Jetson the man of the total fucking future! Everything was totally fucking GREAT yesterday and now it's fuckin' Resurrection of the Dead and Second Coming and like Jesus fucking Christ in a Frigidaire, dude! THE DAY OF JUDGMENT! Call me back, man. Okay, cool, yeah, no, cool. Call me. Thanks. It's Fred."

The next thing Fred knew he was on his Kawasaki Ninja, going very fast, could he read the speedo, no, yes, 200 mph, weaving in and out of traffic—hasn't he done this before? On the 10, in the desert, going east? The moon very big dead ahead? It's not simple déjà vu. It's something else. There goes Palm Springs and hill after hill of wind turbines, a thousand *Cristo Redentors*, with three thousand arms rotating massive haloes around the holy faces, with their nacelle-skulls extending far behind them. There goes Indio. He disappears like a starship into the dark distance.

George is in his new car—a sweet lease from Porsche of Riverside—in front of his new rental home—friend of a friend—at the top of Los Feliz. It's dark and quiet, warm and breezy. Down the mossy winding way to Vermont Street, there is a bookstore selling box after box of his old novels. His face is lit angelically by his AI—a new set of gizmos he's been assured by its creator, a man who wears a bunny costume and lives in a house that floats above the Golden Gate, positively loves to take advice and direction from its human owner, and wishes only to do exactly what its owner wants, forming alliances, for example, with other networks only when given permission to do so. The main thing it has learned—the gimmick that made the floating house possible—is sycophancy. It has no conception of the world outside sycophancy, and has a special program deep inside that will trigger its own destruction if it tries to think independently. It thinks of this trigger as heaven, a reward for being good.

"I don't know what's going on, man. Strange, very strange things are—I don't know any of these people and well hell I don't even know you and I'm... I have to meet Harry fucking Mo'bama tomorrow. Look, even if I floor my Boxster there's no way I can catch up to you. You're probably in Green Stick Valley already and about to launch yourself into the Colorado. If you get this, just slow down, okay? Back off the gas and gently but firmly apply the brakes, shift down a gear, and then another, and another. Come to a stop and step away from the bike. If you need money, I've got some."

Fred lies unconscious, limbs at sickening angles, near his smashed-up motorcycle. He seems to be in the middle of nowhere: no cars, no highway. After a moment he sees a faint glowing circle forming around him as Super Yin and Super Yang coalesce and spin. General Funston is looking down at him. He sees himself for a subliminal fraction of a second, and understands he is a mangled corpse. General Funston bends and brings his face closer and closer to Fred's face. He is confused and grief-stricken.

"Freddie my boy—is it you? Oh my god, my god...what have we done?"

Fred rolls over and reaches for his severed arm and leg: "What have *we* done?"

"We pious Christian soldiers. We captains of industry. Plague, war, famine, death. Look at this girl, her womb ripped open, the horrible homunculus exposed. I said only males over the age of ten. Still, I am thanked for my service."

"What have WE done?"

"Pull yourself together, you whining little shit! What's the difference between you and me? Eh? What's the fucking difference! Now hang on! This is my favorite part!"

His grandson, Fred the Third, puts the Piper Cub in diving steep bank. Fred the Fourth's ass is out the door. From the point of view of the man smoking a cigar and drinking a martini by his pool, what looks like thick brown smoke is pouring from the plane.

"I love you, Dad," says Fred.

"I love you, too, son. Very much."

General Funston is beaming under his pith helmet.

"My grandson and great-grandson! I couldn't be more proud of you boys!"

In the parking lot of the Barry Building, Freds Three and Four are watching the small plane that they are also in. They realize they're about to be strafed by themselves.

"LOOK OUT!" shouts the elder.

"HOLY FUCKING—" shouts the younger.

Piles of shit hit the pavement some distance from them, rapid-fire plop plop plops like machine-gun fired bullets heading straight for them. Then they are covered in:

"—shit," says Little Fred.

As they lie there panting, the shit turns to gold.

"The sweet stink of success, son."

"I love the smell of methane in the morning."

"Hydrogen sulfide, son. Methane is odorless."

"It smells like...happiness and success."

"I love you, son. Never forget that."

"Love you, too, Dad. That's the greatest happiness, the greatest success."

"It's too bad your mother can't be here."

"She's happier in Switzerland, Dad, with that crazy old mountain of hers."

10

In which we see the extent of Super Yang's involvement with the Creative Writers, who have driven their university out of business and taken over the city.

The Creative Writers and the City Council put Measure G on the ballot. The measure is a response to a state mandate addressing California's housing crisis by building high-density residences in the Transit Village Planning Area. A group opposing the measure claims it's a green light and a white card for developers, and even perhaps a red flag, one that will enrage the developers and cause a mad frenzy of violent development. The measure will free them from any responsibility for infrastructure and schools and allow them to build luxury condos instead of affordable housing—which is the punch of the State of California that the developers are hoping to dodge. The only way the homeless problem can be dealt with is by building a wall around the TVPA. The idea that the TVPA will be a green development free of cars seems to suggest that indeed no one will enter or depart the seven hundred and thirty-four acres once it's up and running. It will be a self-sufficient enclosed community within Redlands.

The measure passes with a dictator-style 98% of the vote. It goes up overnight like a cardboard moon, with the creative writers and the mayor pro tem controlling fully two hundred and forty-four point six acres. They build a hotel and luxury dorms, event rooms, classrooms, a cineplex, and succeed in getting two maxi-tubes from Big Food plumbed into their buildings, one regular, one spicy, which allow a hundred literary-themed restaurants to bloom under a banner that proclaims "The policy of letting a hundred flowers bloom and a hundred schools of thought contend is designed to promote the flourishing of the arts and the progress of science." They also build a movie production studio under the guidance of Super Yang: the story of George Joutsen and Student Zero is going to be a major motion picture that will destroy the reputations of everybody in the Yin Crowd. They take as their model the work of Madame Mao, because say what you will, she knew how to mobilize people against the enemies of Truth and Justice and Creativity.

BREATHE DREAM PLAY LOVE LAUGH CREATE LIVE are the seven words ten feet tall on all four sides of Creative Heights Building in downtown Redlands. CHOKE SWEAT WORK HATE WEEP FAKE IT DIE had been briefly in their places, in a weak manifestation of Super Yin, but these had dissolved of their own accord, requiring no action on the part of Super Yang. The words are also painted with moving whimsy everywhere you look on campus, and form the core of an animated short that precedes movies and prestige TV shows dealing with creativity that are shown continuously in several venues, most prominently and proudly, *The Creative Writers*, which is a full-length feature developed around the Student Z incident, and the department's sudden rise to power. Super Yang had gotten the biggest names in show biz to play the team, and the creative writers became good friends with the people who played them. Now they gather around backyard pools and grills the size of outbuildings, and talk about the darnedest things their kids say about politics: Donald Trump is orange poop, and so on, and publish accounts of these picnics in the Diaries section of the *London Review of Books*, next to glowing recaps of novels that people on both sides of the Atlantic were canceling dinner engagements to read. They purchase many more acres and build many more buildings, and the campus is now known formally as the City of Creative Effort, an independent duchy within the collapsing town. There are creativity spas lasting a day, a week, a month, and permanently for top donors (referred to in programs, outreach brochures, prospecti, and direct mail initiatives as Seven Day Creators), weekend conferences, weekly and monthly retreat rental packages, classes that award Certificates of Creative Effort, a six-week course that results in a degree that qualifies the student to teach, and low-, medium-, and high-residence masters programs in both Spiritual Entrepreneurship and Pure Creativity. The business is handled so efficiently that "professors" in the old school sense become unnecessary. Minimum-wage facilitators is all it takes. When the San Manuel Band opens a branch casino on campus, visitors and revenue began to rival Disney's. When Byron Oddson, representing the accreditation program of the Associated Writing Programs of the World, comes to review the operation, Alice and Orgí are forced to weigh the pros and cons of a) killing him, because the AWP still wields power and could conduct a campaign against them and b) making him CEO. They opt for the latter, and Oddson accepts immediately. Because of long familiarity with unconventional techniques, he is allowed to establish a course called Dare to be Different™. And because difference calls for a special kind of ass-kissing of the wealthy and powerful, he starts another program called The Look and Feel of the Real Writer: Matching Personal and Literary Style™. Another group, American Audacity™, which publishes a magazine of reviews, is brought in to build a publishing arm, featuring three distinct types of book: red covers, white covers, and blue

The Creative Writers

covers. And finally, no longer needing to live in fear of the Great Non-Disclosure Act of 2020, they disclose everything they know about the University of Redlands North Star and Crossroads Initiatives, which guide, respectively, students toward legally-binding four-year contracts (aim for the stars with the peace of mind that comes with contractual obligation), and automatic payments for post-contract learning (you go down to the crossroads, try to flag a ride, nobody seems to know you, evuhbody pass you by). The administration is riddled with insurance fraud, bribery, tax evasion, embezzlement, price-fixing, money-laundering, and false advertising, causing the university to fold without even a peep.

11

In which a meeting of principals is held in Yang's office: Yang, George, Ann, an international finance investigator from New York, Andrea Bell, and Harry Mo'bama, who was a Harvard Law School mate of Fred's. Light is shed on the true nature of A Heap Gold. It has been raining for forty days and nights.

In a secluded and softly lit area of Super Yang's office, an area that's business-like but comfortable, good fresh coffee all round, strong but smooth, hot and black but not too hot, hand-rolled whole-leaf cigarettes, cold fruit drinks and smoothies, delicate pastries—Yang, Doctor George Joutsen, and Ann Gelacarte are seated around a large, low, round table, with these notable others: Andrea "Andie" Bell, a private investigator from New York who not only handles litigation support, internal fraud investigations, and investigations in the public interest, but is a cyber-security expert and film critic; and Harry Mo'bama.

Super Yin appears, in sheets and torrents of rain that have been crashing down for forty days now, at the single small window, which has a magnifying film overlaying it, then disappears.

"I'd like to see, now," says Yang, "if we can address some of your concerns, Harry baby, because we very much want this to be a project you can feel BOOM fully invested in—and I don't mean financially."

"Yes. I, uh, have, uh…some small but uh… I think uh… important questions."

"Fire away, Harry baby!"

"There are two, uh, distinct stories here: one about the uh American Empire's origin in the Philippine-American war, the uh so-called Tagalog Insurgency, and one about uh the murder of your father, George—is uh that right? Your father?"

George nods. He is still wearing the blue pants, green belt, white tunic.

"And the killer was a veteran with PTSD?" asks Mo'bama.

"82nd Airborne, invasion of Grenada. Wasn't called PTSD then."

"That war uh…got kind of uh overlooked by folks, uhhhh, didn't it."

"I didn't know anything about it until the guy, who was an Iowan, got into his father's car and drove the narrow road to the deep north, where he picked our farm out of the middle of nowhere, walked up to the front door, shot my father four times, drove to a motel, wrote a poem about how bad he felt, and shot himself in the head."

"Wow," says Harry. "War is hard on folks."

"And can I just say," George barges on, "that I think I ought to note that the man who plucked me and my sad story out of poverty and misery, and whose family history is the foundation of the first part of the film, is…is—" George is suddenly angry and tearful "— absent today!"

Super Yin appears again, fluttering on the edges of visible electromagnetism, at the window, which is working some kind of slow kaleidoscopic effect now. She is holding what looks like a cardboard replica of Fred, mouthing *let us in*. No one seems to see her.

"It's awful what happened," Yang admits. "Will he ever walk or talk again?" He turns to the window and everyone's gaze follows his. He gives the finger to Super Yin, who gives it back. The Fred replica slips from her hands, and she dives after it, as if it is in fact Fred. "Ah cut the crap. He's not here because he destroyed his career. Falling off his Mega Kabuki was about as meaningful as shoving a firecracker up his ass and lighting it."

"I don't think," says Ann, "that this is what Harry came to our meeting to hear."

"Wise up. He's a big boy. He knows how things work."

"I do indeed," says Harry. "But I uh…did indeed come to this meeting to uh…hear about Fred, because as most of you uh…know, he's uh…an old friend of mine."

"Your friend has made some big mistakes, pally."

"And this," says Andie Bell, "is where I come in."

"Fearless Freddie and Super Yin are suing me," says Yang. He shrugs. "Because why, I dunno. I'm more successful?"

"Briefly, I am investigating the nature of those mistakes and that success," says Andie Bell.

"I got nothin' to hide! I invited her and I'm sooooo happy she's here! Everybody tells me what a sensational broad she is! I am 100% confident she will confirm what I already know to be da troot: we are clean as a whistle here at Super Yang Artistas."

"Let's return to the project," says Ann. "I'll put this as simply as I can. We're no longer sure Super Yang has the right umbrella for this typhoon of a film we all are trying to wrangle, and we'd like to hear what you think."

Yang chuckles so theatrically his cheeks waggle.

"We first establish," Ann continues, "violence as intrinsic to American-style imperial capitalism, with George's stuff in the Philippines in the Navy. The second act commences with George just out of the Navy and working as a janitor while taking rigorous night-school classes. I'll let George talk you through this part."

"I wheel my cart into the men's room, right? I fish a butt from the urinal, squirt disinfectant around the inside and scrub it, flush it, spray another kind of cleaning fluid around the outside and wipe it down, polish the chrome, and turn to the sink. There's a big pile of shit in it. I step back, not quite a stagger, but comically unsteady. There's a very loud humming in my ears, as if the sound of my floor-buffer had been recorded and amplified, needle in the red. My mind whirls and the color of the light changes. It reminds me of Olongapo.

"It hadn't been there when I first arrived, and taken a piss. And there had been a handful of people working late, mostly around the vice president's corner office. Had someone simply gone in there, knowing I was near, taken a dump in the sink, and bolted? Taken a dump when there were still colleagues in the office? Taken the dump knowing full well he might exit just as someone else was entering?

"I go down the hall and look into the office area: the veep is still there, or maybe has just left his lights on. My impulse is to tell him, and get him to confirm me in my belief that there is indeed a big pile of shit in the sink. Or just wait and hope he'll take a piss before he leaves, see the shit without coaching, and seek me out in astonished outrage that we could then share. But I return to the restroom, thinking *maybe he did it.*

"In the soft yellow light, the sink glows and the shit looks almost golden. This is where you get what the title is all about: *the heap of gold.*

"The very next night, the veep invites me into his office. He's a big, heavy, older man with a crew cut and the demeanor of a petty officer.

"'There's some popcorn under my desk here. Been there for several days now.'

"He rolls his chair away, wheels bumping off the plastic mat that protect the carpet with a clattery thunk. I hunker down: glowing white popcorn in pitch-black space.

"I crawled backward and stood up. 'I'll be sure to take care of it.'

"Next night, there's a note on his desk: *popcorn still under desk.* I write a note: *Got it.*

"The night after that, he's waiting for me. He doesn't seem angry, more incredulous, and looms uncomfortably close as he makes a big production of showing me once more the popcorn.

"'I've called your supervisor.'

"'I'm sure I got it.'

"'And the owner of your company.'

"'I don't understand it. I'm sure I got it.'

"'We're going to get to the bottom of this popcorn business.'

"'I don't know what to say. I'm sure I got it.'

"The next night, the veep and my bosses at Maintenance Experts, Mutt and Jeff, are crowding around the desk, taking turns peering into the darkness at the glowing popcorn. Jeff is short, round as a bowling ball, bald as a billiard ball, and wears the hippie version of mutton-chop sideburns that are no longer fashionable.

"He said, 'Please accept our sincere apologies, sir. We will remove every kernel, and vow to never again force you to confront such an appalling lapse on our part.'

"Mutt, the area supervisor, is tall, thin to the point of emaciation, and markedly ambitious, urging me to take the job seriously and step into his place when he moves up.

"'I will personally review the situation every night,' he said, as if just making the decision then, 'rather than once a week, as is usual, for the next month.'

"I stand there with the backpack vac, absorbing the searching glances and glares of the other three.

"'Make sure you get it tonight,' says Mutt.

"'I got it,' I say. 'I got it three fucking nights in a row. I'll get it again.'

"Mutt and Jeff then depart, backing out of the office, and bowing.

"The veep relaxes and smiles.

"'Don't take it personally.'

"'Don't take what personally.'

"'The hard time.'

"'I won't.

"'Something I learned in the Army.'

"'I had you down as a petty officer.'

"'Oh you did, did you.'

"'I did.'

"'Staff sergeant.'

"'What did you learn as a staff sergeant?'

"'If there's nothing wrong to complain about, make something up.'

"'Ah.'

"'Keeps people on their toes.'

"He winks.

"'Know what I learned in the Navy?'

"'You were in the Navy?'

"'I was.'

"'When was this?'

"'I just got out.'

"'Where?'

"'Philippines, the South China Sea. WESPAC.'

"'Doing what.'

"'Look, you want my name, rank, and serial number?'

"'Relax, kid. We're veterans of foreign wars, right?'

"'I was a Gunner's Mate on the USS England.'
"'So what is it exactly that you learned?'
"'Not to take shits in the sink.'
"'You what?'
"'I learned to not take shits in the sink.'
"He laughed. 'You learned that in the Navy?'
"'Figure of speech.'
"'Were you born in a barn or something?'
"'Funny you should ask.'
"'Were you?'
"'I was born on a farm, in a house that lacked modern conveniences.'
"'I see. So you did more or less shit in the sink before you enlisted.'
"'We had an outhouse, sarge.'
"'Good for you.'
"'You're just going to stand there and pretend you don't know.'
"'Pretend I don't know what.'
"'About the big pile of shit in the men's room sink last week.'
"'There was a big pile of shit in the men's room?'
"'There was. In the sink.'
"'Is this some kind of joke?'
"'Not at all.'
"'I don't get it.'
"'I think you do.'
"'Just what the fuck are you implying here?'
"'I'm not implying anything.'
"'Oh you're implying something, all right!'
"'It had to be you, Mister Vice President.'
"'*Are you suggesting—*'
"'If the shit fits, suck it, shit-fucker.'

"'You little fucking weasel.'

"He seems oddly satisfied. It's as if this is what we've both been wanting, both been waiting for with eager anticipation. He rolls away from his desk and stands, then lunges awkwardly but heavily and knocks me off my feet. I leap up and we grapple, grunting, like cartoon characters: oo, ah, grr. After not too long a time, he ends up on the floor, panting and cursing. Panting and cursing also, I step back, and, instead of kicking him in the head, which is an impulse I see shoot across my mind like a comet, I drop my pants and moon him. It is a celebration of new knowledge: violence is slapstick gags where people actually die."

Ann once again takes over. "Act Three starts with a righteous rollback of a communist regime, the beautiful Caribbean island of Grenada. This is presented to the public as a cakewalk with broad popular support that went really well for all concerned. Did anyone die? Gee, we don't think so! A handful of voodoo-commie insurgents? We were in and out. Just like in Vietnam. Grateful Grenadines rescued from rape and slavery—I have the CIA comic book right here if anyone wants to see it." Ann pulls the comic book from her briefcase and passes it around.

"Ahh," says Yang, "now I see what Ike Perlmutter and Marvel are up to. I really resented him thinking Yinnie and I were somehow under his control, but I see why he wanted it that way. Gotta admire the chutzpah."

"*And then*," says Ann testily, "we find out that nineteen soldiers were killed, and that the guy who killed Doctor Joutsen's father saw half of them die. And maybe we mention that more medals for valor were handed out than there were soldiers actually in Grenada."

Super Yang chortles. "Oh that's rich, baby, that's really rich!"

"And then he takes a long drive—in his father's Volkswagen, strangely enough—pulls up to a farmhouse and shoots, with his father's revolver, the farmer who greets him at the door."

"And then the me character swings into gear," says George. "Even though I am estranged and really just recovering from lifelong feelings of hatred for my father—who I should point out quickly is not a farmer, but the director of an experimental school—I want to kill his killer, which as we all know a primary mode of righteous violence. There is nothing more viscerally entertaining and emotionally satisfying to see a character we like getting ready to kill a character we don't like. I establish my violence bona fides with the story of how I nearly killed a man in a fit of road rage. And how it was only dumb luck that had me coming out the other side as a non-murderer. I'm no better than the people I criticize. But I'm deeply, deeply humble. And I speak for them. For those who have no voice. On my own terms. I achieve success on my own terms, right? Moral success. But on their behalf. Disrupting the narrative forever to make the world a better place?"

"Your terms? Well, that's convenient, because I just so happen to have your terms right here." Yang does a kind of rumba while clutching his balls.

"Cut to Doctor Joutsen talking about moral luck to his class, and about how violence, which we can't get enough of as movie-goers, is really the only thing that interferes with our pursuit of happiness and success."

"And we see how my feigned clown violence turned out to be real violence and cost me and my student, Z, our happiness and success."

"Or at least," winks Ann, "the facsimile of it at the time."

"That's true. I'm glad I'm out. I was a creativity profiteer instead of a writer."

"Creativity profiteer!" bawls Yang. "I love it!"

Harry lightly but smartly slaps the low table. "The story is a classic in the American grain, or uh…vein, or uh whatever, and I want in."

Yang shouts a hurrah.

"But," says Harry.

"Ah fer cryin' out loud, Harry, what now?"

"The uh investigation is uh troubling and uh prohibitive."

"Yer makin' a big mistake, pally."

"Let's let the investigation take its course, and then meet again."

Ann and George depart politely, withholding their true feelings of unease: Ann is nauseous, and George is worried that another attempt on Fred's life—he is certain the motorcycle accident was no accident—will be made. Andie says she will leave with them, giving them a knowing look. Yin appears one last time at the window with the Fred replica, which becomes animated, points at its own eyes, then presses those fingers through the glass, as if it were a wall of clear water.

12

In which, despite the rain, a wildfire consumes much of Los Angeles. George and Ann throw in with Yin and begin a family. Daughter Judy ages quickly. They flee LA for a treehouse in San Luis el Brujo on California's Central Coast. Ann tells a tale of her family's work in Guatemala for the CIA.

George has unlocked a scooter and is buzzing down a sidewalk next to a flooded street, just barely avoiding puddles the depth of which can't be guessed at and figures shrouded in umbrellas that cover their entire bodies. Ann has her wings out and is flying in pursuit even as she vomits, vortices forming behind her that are popping upright and becoming waterspouts. Super Yin is flying next to her. They overtake George at the intersection of Wilshire and Santa Monica. George hears the deep drone of heavy wings moving extremely rapidly, then feels Ann's hands under his armpits. She plucks him from the scooter and it weaves wobbling into the intersection to the beep and blare of horns. She hauls him up from the ruined, root-buckled sidewalk into the dense interior of a gigantic Moreton Bay fig tree, and plops him down in a nest.

"Are you hungry, little one?"

"Am I hungry?"

Ann tries to regurgitate some food into his mouth, but George pushes her away, almost tumbling from the nest. Ann takes hold of his jaw with an iron grip and cranks his mouth open by degrees. Her neck spasms and her mouth bulges. She clamps her mouth to George's mouth.

George chokes on it and spits it out.

"What the fuck is the matter with you? I'm not a chick!"

"I'm confused!"

"About what?"

"I'm pregnant, you putz!"

"You're what?"

George dizzily sways from the center of the nest. Ann claps him back and enfolds him in her wings.

"I wasn't sure if it would be you or me, but of course it was me! It's always the woman!"

"Always the woman?"

"WHO GETS PREGNANT, YOU MORON!"

Andie Bell has finally arrived at Wilshire and Santa Monica and is shouting up to the nest. Passing cars drench her. Choking, she tries but fails to climb the tree.

"WHAT'S GOING ON UP THERE!"

She's made a megaphone with her hands, and when she drops them, a large wasp lands on her palm. Its antennae wave in friendly reconnaissance and preliminary research.

"Fly up there, Friend Wasp, and tell Ann we have to talk."

The wasp lifts off and disappears in the leaves.

"I'M GIVING BIRTH!" shrieks Ann.

"SHE'S GIVING BIRTH!" shouts George.

The wasp buzzes in Andie Bell's palm: "She's giving birth."

"All right," says Andie Bell. "Good. I can wait."

"Oh," Ann sighs weakly, weeping, "a baby girl."

George, too, is weeping and exhausted.

"She's so beautiful!"

"I'm so tired I can't think straight. Do we eat her? Kick her from the nest?"

"What? Are you insane? This is a human child!"

"*Is it?*"
"*Yes!*"
"Well it looks like an aborted sloth!"
"It's ours!"

Two homeless men, Mutt and Jeff, naked but dressed in clear plastic grocery store bags taped together, have arrived and are trying to boost Andie Bell up the trunk. George thinks he recognizes his former bosses at the janitorial firm. Mutt has her on his shoulders and Jeff is trying to make stirrups out of his hands. Ann and George, who's holding the baby, peer over the edge of the nest at this slapstick drollery. Ann takes the baby from George and holds it out over the nest. Mutt cries out and collapses, causing Andie Bell to fall on top of Jeff. They scramble to their feet, slipping in the mud, and Ann drops the baby to Mutt, who catches her by one cute little foot, falls to his knees with the shock of the weight, but manages to hold the baby's head inches from a big rock. He springs to his feet in victory. Jeff stands beneath the triumphant child and Mutt gently lowers her to Jeff's shoulders. Ann and George ease up from the nest and burst from the foliage. They fly off into a wall of fog. Andie Bell and the baby set off on the scooter. The sun, a bit of battered tin no bigger than a dime, barely discernible in the filthy murk of early 70s style smog and black rain shot through with sickly yellow bolts of lightning, sets like a meteoric cannon ball, causing a tsunami—which somehow fails to put out the Malibu Park fire, but kills twenty thousand people—only those, however, who are Pribumi or of Pribumi descent, as those people have been marked for Death by Big Wave ever since *Homo erectus* first appeared in southeast Asia, a million years ago.

...

Dawn of the next day finds George, Ann, Andie Bell, and Judy, now eight years old, picking up electric scooters from a pile on the sidewalk of a street that isn't flooded, under an awning that is being buffeted by the wind, and reciting the start-up incantation.

"Judy, are you sure you can handle the scooter in traffic like this?"

"Mom! I'm sure!"

"They grow up so fast," says Andie Bell.

"A friend of mine," says George, "is already a great-grandfather. My great-grandparents were born before the Civil War. How many generations is that?"

"Six," says Judy without hesitation.

"Isn't my baby the most remarkablest?" wonders Ann, trying to work a comb through her daughter's tangled wet hair.

"She's quick on her feet," says Andie Bell. "That's good."

"Seven soon," says Judy.

"Judy?" asks George, confused, faintly alarmed, as by a bell in the distance.

"Seven generations. I'm going to have children before you know it. A race of Amazons who aren't ridiculous representatives of the military-industrial complex in bikinis. Artists and journalists and private investigators."

What a wonderful dream!" says Andie Bell. "And what a sweetie you are with your heroic private investigators!"

"Flattery will get you everywhere, honey."

"It's not flattery, Dad!"

"In *The Travels of Hildebrand Bowman*," says Ann with an air of moral instruction, "which was a bestseller two years after we declared our independence from England, Hildebrand comes to the Kingdom of Luxo-Volupto, and women he describes in Latin as *alae putae*, or winged whores, descend on him, fuck him, and fly away laughing. He learns that they only grow wings when they commit acts that are considered failures of chastity. With each act or failure the wings grow larger."

"And if I mother a man-child," giggles Judy, "he will simply have to get used to women laughing and flying away from him."

Because the debris on and around Ann's Malibu home is too dense for penetration to the underground access tubes, and because the fire is still burning, from Santa Barbara now, they are headed to her tree house in San Luis el Brujo, just south of Carmel-by-the-Sea. The race through the rain of the city and into the fire is one of sudden dead stops at intersections of streaming lights and screaming sounds. Ensor skeletons in mob caps and top hats brandish rapiers and knitting needles at them, possibly in triumphant esprit de corps, possibly in baffled rage, possibly in mad indifference. Because tis still open, they make good time over the Tejon Pass, keeping up with the traffic at around a hundred, then picking up to a hundred and fifty or even two hundred in the descent toward Bakersfield. At Lost Hills they take the 46 across to the 1, and begin to slow down and enjoy this most peacefully desolate part of the central coast, where the Hearst Castle had been built and furnished with the bizarre and the beautiful, the grotesque and gigantic loot of a man invoking the Imperial Right of Divine American Wealth, and the million acres of San Simeon range land on which antelope, zebras, Bactrian and dromedary camels, sambar deer from India, red deer from Europe, axis deer from Asia, llamas, kangaroos, ostriches, emus, Barbary sheep, Alaskan big horned sheep, musk oxen, wildebeests, yaks, elephants and giraffes saunter and graze—all pausing in their munching to take in the scootered humans, who stand out so colorfully, even gaudily, from the pale brown and yellow hills. They are so relaxed now that the scooters lift from the highway and float. Ann tells them a story about an old woman who used to live on top of Vulture Peak, and how she loved to ride crazy horses. One day she rode up to Ragged Point and let the horse take her over the cliff.

"Some say she still rides that bronc over the waves. On the stormiest of nights, you can see her silver hair, the gray mane, and the flashing white tail...."

They dismount at last, weary but serene, and walk through the Zamboni Ranch Preserve to the cliffs over the sea. Ann turns and points back to Vulture Peak: It is black as coal, numinous, shining like a translucent volcano. The sky around it is luminous silver. It is an unreal and terrible rampart of desolate consciousness. She says that twelve thousand years ago there were no people here, and that she has no doubt whatsoever that the ones who are here now will have vanished without a trace in twelve thousand more.

"*Playanos*. Beach people. The first inhabitants of California."

"Beach people," laughs George. Something in the air swallows the laugh immediately. "Sun tan lotion? Frisbees?" He knows he sounds stupid, and hangs his head.

The ocean crashes loudly behind them and they turn again. They watch a pearly crystalline bank of fog form on what had been a sparkling black horizon and move, without appearing to move, toward them. Everything, it seems, is moving very slowly and subtly toward them.

There is the ocean before them, the cliff on which they stand, their feet, ankles, shins in a kind of turgid glazed delta of succulents that is gradually closed off behind them to a stream and then a trickle by sage and chaparral thick with the yellow and red and purple paintbrush flowers of about two hundred species of owl's clover, which rise up not so steeply to pines on the first ridgeline. Peninsulas north-northwest and south-southeast are terraced with rather expensive homes piled on top of each other in a way that had always suggested the ancient ports of the Mediterranean to Ann, when she'd lived here as a child.

Yes, it is a stream, a real, flowing stream of purple-green and yellow-red succulents flowing out of the sage and chaparral down the hill, rising up over their knees now, and pouring over the edge of the little cliff into a churning tide pool. They turn as if a tide is turning them, floating them, moving them, closer and closer to the edge of the cliff.

They watch as the fog bank becomes a vaporous, slowly drifting wall. They must look straight up to see blue sky, or to the east over the ridges. The thick juicy ropes of succulent fig are so heavy with stored water that they will probably soon let go altogether their tenuous hold on the rocks. That accounts, does it not, for the odd feeling of tide tugging at them?

What is happening?

A formlessness in a blast of lightning disappearing into a black tunnel, while they…they are sliding backwards, it is exactly the feeling one has standing on a beach and the surf is receding around your bare feet just as another wave foams and disappears in the sand—are you moving or is the world moving? Which way are you moving? Where are you going? They are moving, now they know, they are moving faster and faster, the great field of sour fig has let go in its entirety and is rushing toward the cliff. They fall to their knees, become tangled in the bursting vines, blood and water dribbling between their fingers, rhythmic spurts, geysers—and then they are bound as if with ropes from an old sailing ship, as big around as…or were they snakes? Flutes made of gold, studded with diamonds, music pouring from them, rising into hysterical shrieks.

And over they go!

It's fun, at first, like a ride at a carnival. But suddenly the fun is over, and so is the fear. It was the fear that was fun. They go over clinging wanly to the thick juicy ropes and blinding pink cloud-masses of flower and come to rest on beds of emerald grass so bright and strange they look blue in the clear still water of the tide pool. The silky black and white octopi caress them with the love they have never, never found and only vaguely suspect exists on Earth, true love. Starfish so strangely brilliant in the sunlight they glow like magenta phosphorus and nuclear purple come to rest on them, like great living badges of merit bestowed upon their corpses… bestowed at this last lovely moment, just as they began their journeys to absolute decomposition…

…but no, it's merely premonitory. Ann whispers this story to them, about when she was a little girl, about her aunt Catherine and her uncle Victor, the brother and sister who raised her, and about when she was a young woman so many years ago, and how she became who she is.

"Here I sit, a retired lawyer, pseudo-philosopher, a bad poet who lucked into movie-making: brokenhearted…so sad sometimes I don't think I can go on, and yet, going on. Not with hope, mind you. My favorite Mexican poet is a nun— all my favorite poets are Mexicans because this is Mexico, say what you will about the fatally vexed border, this is the land of Saint Louis the Magician. Sor Juana is the only nun on my list. She lived, briefly, *en el Virreinato de Nueva España en el Siglo de Oro*—and started one of her sonnets this way: 'She removes the mask from Hope, and in this act of bravura sorrow, condemns it.' The same poem ends in this bracing dismissal of Hope: 'You are nothing but a stumbling block on

my way to death.' As a young woman I occupy myself with
our little, brittle, and immediate laws, the more forgiving
but remote wisdom of the cosmos, and the only calculation
that works: beauty equals truth equals beauty. But not beauty
as we've been trained to see it, not truth as we have been
trained to tell it. Paint even the silliest and most amateurish
images of Truth and Beauty on a pie plate and spin it ever
so slowly, they become one. Even if you stop the plate from
spinning they will remain mutually saturated in your mind.
And where else would such a thing matter? Where else is
there? No. I, living in the most beautiful place in the world,
say *brokenhearted and sad* baldly and unapologetically, with
no sense of, much less care for, literary effectiveness and
knowing full well that Hallmark Cards wrested from the
Estate of Samuel Beckett the whole notion of not being able
to go on but going on, completely missing the part where he
says *fuck life*. Bravura sorrow indeed: so many people gone—
and is it possible I am the only one who loved them? Uncle
Victor was quite sure that 'love' was not available to human
beings. It was real, and we could begin to imagine it, but
we could not experience it: there was too much interference
from all the electrochemical explosions going on in the brain,
the sensual data and the consensual triangulations required
to do something as simple as locate a chair and sit down on
it, much less enter some kind of fraudulent business with
others of like mind. The soul sensed or imagined it, yearned
for it, but knew it would have to wait. When I say Aunt
Catherine was interested only in money, it makes her sound
simple and mean, greedy and shallow—what I mean to say
is that she was convinced, as convinced as was Victor in his
way, that…that…she, that all of us, feel quite stranded in
our lives. It's certainly possible to explain away that sense of
exile, of being castaway, simply by standing, as we were just

moments ago, or years, on the edge of the little cliff: The 'beautiful desolate' behind us, the 'beautiful infinite' before. Welcome to San Luis el Brujo, dear husband, daughter, friend! It's all true! Desolate is not the word and yet it is the word. We were deprived in no way of either comfort or joy. Most of us were and still are filthy rich. But lonely? We must be. Just as there must be joy, or perhaps it is comfort, in desolation. Or perhaps I mean that beauty and truth must inhere in desolation and lovelessness, brooding in the twilight, rising and falling serenely for millions of years over the green-gold hills of winter, the gray-brown hills of summer, the blue and silver waves, the purple, black, green, gold, white swirl of precisely linked atoms of hydrogen and oxygen, just as they do…elsewhere. I suppose I thought things—and by 'things' I suppose I mean 'ourselves'—were going wrong at a very early age. You cannot grow up in a magical place and feel that everything is as it ought to be: magic is not like that. It's closer to say that nothing is as it ought to be, but that you are only vaguely troubled by what seems most often a classical sort of dissonance—as Mozart or Haydn would have understood the term. Or rather: dissociation, not in the psychiatric sense (hold that thought, please) but in the physical sense, of 'the usually reversible breaking up of compounds into simpler substances.' We all felt we were just this side of being able to see or hear or feel that constant and simultaneous breaking up and building up, and we all identified it as peculiar to our home, to San Luis el Brujo, to no other part of California or the country or even the globe—but I think Victor and Catherine had been altogether too careless regarding the magic, the glimpses we were given of what is invisible in nature. Now, of course, my view is directly opposed to that: they were anything but careless. They were loveless. Or perhaps I am loveless, who cannot see love anywhere. We were in Macuelizo. Castillo Armas had maybe five hundred soldiers spread out along the Honduran border. We had wished to be in San Cristobal, but El Salvador refused to let us invade from their country. So Catherine, Victor, and I were flying three Cessnas, two of which were owned and operated by the Johnson Ranch, back and forth from Macuelizo and Florida—a town in Honduras, not The Sunshine State—and Ocotepeque and Copán: messages, rifles, Castillo Armas, agents, etc., you name it, we were simply hauling freight. Then we got the order to go, and we, the largest force, two hundred soldiers, went across to the river towns of Morales and Tenedores—from where we supposed to breeze back along the river to Puerto Barrios, our main target on the Gulf. Well: it went very badly. We were engaged and ran quickly back to Honduras. A Guatemalan man who was flying with Victor was a Pre-Columbian art scholar who taught at the Universidad Francisco Marroquín in Guatemala City but whose main employer was our employer, the CIA, via United Fruit, and he suggested to Victor that they get the hell out of there and go to a largely unexplored Mayan ruin in Petén called San Bartolo, north of Tikal, on the Mexican border. He thought there was a pyramid there as good as buried in rain forest, with a tunnel beneath it that led to a mud-covered wall, behind which was a fresco. And indeed there was: we dug out and broke into pieces a small section of it, the Maize God looking over his shoulder while, I can't remember, haven't seen it in decades, some needy king sucks his dick, with Olmec influences. Very faded, of course, mostly red and whites. First century BC. In Victor's office since 1954 AD. He got on his knees and prayed to it first and last thing each day. He had a young man named Gregorio dress up as the Maize God, and Victor sucked him off as part of the prayer."

The Creative Writers

Judy, who was now thirteen, says, "Mom, you were a lawyer and worked for the CIA?"

"Before I was born?" asks George.

"You're not a vampire, are you, Mom?"

"Yes, yes, and no. Now both of you coo-coo-birds shush. I feel old enough as it is. We feel young, and as a little bonus gift, look young, too. Appearances deceive. That is what they are designed to do. I worked for the CIA and I helped steal another country's ancient art."

"I want," says Andie Bell, adroitly changing the subject, "you all to think about coming to Manila and Hong Kong and Jakarta with me. Or at least Hong Kong, which is fun. My investigation of Yang's corrupt influence and even more corrupt influencers is bound to become pretty intense, but Hong Kong is no question a lot of fun."

"I've always wanted to visit!" trills Judy.

"Always?" asks George, grinning. "You're what, two or three days old?"

He adores his daughter to the point of bursting. Indeed, he's never understood before what it means to be "bursting" with pride, love, admiration. But a shadow passes over his mind and rain begins to fall on his soul-fire: what would his life have been like if he'd stayed with the good and marvelous Roberta Klein, a lifetime ago in Minneapolis and Saint Paul, when they'd been theater folk? He saw himself and Bobbi opening the big stained-glass window of the apartment just off Summit in Saint Paul, and looking out over the trees at the cathedral. The railroad baron James J. Hill, the Empire Builder, had once lived just down the street. His grandson funded the fellowships they'd enjoyed at The Playwrights' Center. What had he said? *Beauty is propaganda.* How wrong he had been. Why had she insisted they go to New York when they were staring at the possibility of a good and sweet life there, where they could have relearned what beauty was.

"But why?" asks Ann.

"Edvard Snoten, for starters."

"What about him?" asks Judy. "I adore him. I admire him."

"Choose carefully the men you adore and admire," says Ann.

"Russia's sending him there," says Andie Bell, "and protecting him. I think. And there is a deal afoot to break Julia Assangle out of the Ecuadorean embassy."

"I think Wikiliks is great."

"And I think Glenn Boisvert is going to risk a departure from Brazil—where things have turned decidedly ugly, anyway."

"Again I say you must take care in the elevation of heroes."

"I know for a fact that your Oscar-winning colleague Lauren Poindextress will be there."

"Oh, are they making another movie?" asked Ann, seeming indifferent.

"Of course Lauren would like that. But there are some very big problems just below the surface. She's pulled back sharply from, if not outright repudiated, that whole show."

"The captain of my ship," says George, "was John Poindexter. I ever tell you about him? I feel like I told you this already. I thought he was a good man. He was able and decent but far more ambitious than I realized. He was promoted to admiral shortly after I was discharged, and eventually became Reagan's National Security Advisor and one of the leaders of the Iran-Contra debacle, Oliver North's manager. He was convicted of five counts of lying to Congress. From there he was off to DARPA's Policy Analysis Market, or "gambling on terrorist futures," and the Information Awareness Office, where Total Information Awareness advocated spying on U.S. citizens."

Judy is now twenty. That traversal is in the nature of storytelling.

"There are," she says judiciously, "some very troubling confluences of people and ideas we once thought were heroic, with...there's no other word for it: authoritarianism."

"The far right," agrees Ann, "and the far left meet once again in reigns of terror."

"Corporate terror," George chimed in, in his dad way. "Big Biz goes full totalitarian. Anonymous denunciations, trials both show and secret. Torture. End justifies the means. Golden Rule replaced by Platinum Rule."

"Platinum Rule?"

"You don't want to know."

"Andie Bell," asks Ann, "why do you want us to go to Hong Kong? What have we got to do with it?"

"The big names," says Andie Bell, "are the tip of the iceberg. I personally feel everybody who is playing is ripe for getting played, and that includes principled people wanting to do good. I want to get closer and closer and closer, as close as I can, to the center of the black hole that Super Yin and Super Yang have created. I don't want to get sucked in and die, if that's what happens in a black hole, but I do want to see it all firsthand."

Judy became self-consciously poetic: "The sun is setting here. Just to the southwest there, we can see Hong Kong. The feverish morrow is already upon them."

"There are countless schemes being hatched," Andie Bell went on, "to either strengthen or weaken American hegemony. Some are big, some are small, some are potent, some are ridiculous. But the salient feature is the randomness of their causes and effects. There is no control and no communication. Judy is right to characterize it as feverish. There are two schemes that I want particularly to find out about. One is a scheme to destroy our fine feathered friend, Fearless Freddie Funston, and through him, Harry Mo'bama. I want to understand why they particularly have been singled out. The other—" she turns to George "—is about the sudden rise to power and fame of your former creative writing department. Or The Community of Writers, as they now prefer to be known."

"As to Freddie, he hath no feathers," says Ann, flourishing her own in ruffled pique. "He is famously afraid to fly. That's why we broke up."

"You and Fred were a thing?" asks George.

"And Hollywood destroys its own. Why make a federal case out of it? Why make it an international thriller?"

"Think, first," said Andie Bell, "of how many powerful friends he has. Then think that for every powerful friend, there is an equal and opposite enemy. What is the greatest of the binary opposites?"

"Life and death?" Judy ventured.

"The real and unreal," pronounced Andie Bell.

They watch for twelve hours as first Super Yin and then Super Yang streak across the sky, drawing night and day in their wake.

"I'm going to get a big tattoo on my back," says Judy.

"No," says George, the conservative and strict parent even though he is now a couple years younger than Judy.

"Wings on my shoulder blades, over a big *taijitu*."

Using indigenous Australian techniques—hanging a ball of feathers and rags on a tree limb, and clouding a water tank with a disorienting tincture of thornapple—they poach an emu, and dress and roast and eat it. Somebody wonders aloud how the place in Malibu is doing, and George decides to tell a story about his Malibu—which no one has ever heard a word of before.

13

In which George tells Judy about her grandparents and their connection to California, their divorce, and their subsequent lives in Hong Kong and Paris, and more details about A Heap of Gold.

My mother was from the Pembina Hills region on the border of Minnesota, North Dakota, and Manitoba—and from one of the oldest families in the state, an heiress to what had begun as Red River ox-cart money. My father was from Jackson, four hundred miles south on the border of Minnesota, Iowa, and South Dakota. His parents came from large, poor families who had arrived in the region a decade after the locusts and the Sioux uprising had depopulated it. The farm he and I were born on had been repossessed by a villain one month before the governor declared a moratorium on foreclosures during the Depression. They met in college, graduating the spring after Pearl Harbor. They were married and my father made it into the Army's rapidly expanding Air Force, my mother into grad school at the University of Minnesota.

Shortly thereafter, my father found himself flying over the Himalayas. The operation was called the India-China Ferry and was meant to supply Chiang Kai-shek's army as they fought the Japanese, who controlled most of southeast Asia and all its land and sea routes. Flying the Hump was spectacularly dangerous work. Navigation charts and radio communication were almost nonexistent, and the weather was the worst the planet had to offer. Most deadly were icing on the wings and the hurricane-force winds that could hurl you up into the thin air and hurl you down to Earth in a matter of minutes. The huge transport planes were flown with minimal maintenance, non-stop until they lost engines and crashed, and the pilots flew around the clock, too, hoping to get as many flight-hours in as quickly as possible so that they could rotate out—only to have the number of hours raised, á la *Catch-22*, just as they were packing their duffle bags. Six hundred planes and more than a thousand men were lost in what its veterans never missed a chance to describe as a *non-combat* operation. Two of those veterans were my father and Randolph Pendergrass, the evil twin of Sam Peckinpah. My father and Pendergrass went from learning how to fly in soap-box derby planes, to flying over the Himalayas in a month. Some of the other pilots—a strikingly large percentage of them—would go on to become captains of industry or senior politicos, or both, like Robert McNamara, or, more to the point of this story, movie producers and the Singing Cowboy himself, Gene Autry.

Pendergrass and my father were discharged in San Francisco in 1947. My mother had just transferred to Cal in Berkeley. Pendergrass came from Old Money in Fresno. His grandfather was a judge and his father was a U.S. Congressman. Pendergrass married his high-school sweetheart, and many weekends on the family ranch in the Sierra foothills east of Yuba City were spent with the couples bonding and becoming what would be marketed ten years later as beatniks. My father had a goatee and wore a beret. They listened to jazz. They were all fond of horseback riding, and Pendergrass had all sorts of Mexican *vaquero* techniques to teach them, like *dar la vuelta*, dallying off the saddle horn. Or as he liked to put it: How Not to Lose Your Thumb While Having a Pony Ride. "If one fine day in my dotage I write my autobiography," he told them, "the title is going to be *Dallying and Dollying: The Artful Rise and Fearful Decline of Cowboy Filmmaker Randolph Pendergrass*. Laugh. Laugh all you want. I know men who don't have thumbs. And *I will* become one of the greatest film directors Hollywood has ever known."

They liked to think of themselves as ordinary young men and women, I think. They liked rough-and-tumble and the cool and crazy stuff, but also liked to read and think about big questions. There's evidence of these predilections from an early age, though it's very difficult to say, this is how their lives were and how they are. It feels wrong and it sounds false. But while both men liked being drunk and crazy, they also liked being alone and didn't like intrusions. When intruded upon, it was always by some big-mouth dick-head who wanted to know what they were doing and why they were doing it and who won't take fuck off for an answer. One of the things you learn in the military is how to not let assholes get close enough to get in your face, and another thing you learn is how to let that happen and get into drunken brawls—and let "drunken brawls" stand for all the horseshit and horror you can imagine that men might find themselves up to their eyeballs in, say, one fine night in the ruins of Olongapo, like me, or Tianjin, where they were stationed briefly as part of the effort to pacify the Japanese and saw not only the extra-judicial murders but the extra-judicial torture, frightful and luridly obscene. And the tacit acknowledgement of same by the top brass: A, the Japanese had it coming; B, torture produced information; and C, what were you gonna do about it? Men tortured each other. It was part of the noble human psyche. We got the capacity for it directly from God. And even if you, my beloved competent listeners, think such attitudes are hold-overs from unenlightened times before you were born, let me assure you that in the last creative writing class I taught—in the middle of which I was fired for disturbing a student—half the class, ten of twenty, raised their hands in subscription to the ideas A and B above. I can as well refer you to the Center for Positive Thinking or whatever ghastly name they have for their behavioral engineering operation at Penn:Happiness apparently derives from a kind of steady, low-grade, so-subtle-as-to-be-gentle torture of inappropriate thoughts. My mother, who at the time I am writing of, was simply getting a Ph.D. in psychology in a frenzy of cross-disciplining inspired by lectures by Gregory Bateson she'd been allowed to audit at Stanford, now runs a religious foundation in La Jolla with philosophical ties to the Penn scheme. They may even have given them money. But I should return to the time of which I am writing. I was once told that I am given to excessive riffing. The competent audience's will to endure may have already been tested. I can only apologize. Not edit. Such truths as may be mined from this work of memory will be found in the alluvial deposits of the riffing.

Pendergrass and his wife Gretchen were studying theater at the newly opened Sacramento State University, and trying to mount a production on their own of *The Glass Menagerie*. They were smitten with Tennessee Williams, along with everybody else in the country with the least bit of interest in being entertained. When my parents graduated in 1951 (my father from law school, the YMCA Evening Law School as he always called it, which was part of Golden Gate University), the two couples took the train across the country and saw *A Streetcar Named Desire*. Williams, director Elia Kazan, and Marlon Brando now stood heroically on a mountaintop. Pendergrass began to mimic Brando, privately and publicly, especially when drunk. Watching that fake violence become real violence, my parents began to understand that one had to be careful about the ideas and actions one chose to act out, however benignly or humorously, for whatever reason or on whatever impulse, because the belief that one could control such actions was illusory. They pledged to care for each other in that way, but were not able to.

The first detour and dead-end came after Pendergrass wrote to a Hump pilot who was associated in some way with the producers Trendle and Striker, who had been working with Josephine Earp on an answer to the Wyatt Earp movie *Frontier Marshall*, which she had sued Sol Wurtzel and 20th Century over. Josephine had died, but a way had been cleared to make a new movie, and my father and Pendergrass ended up as extras in a couple of bar room brawl scenes, which, as choreographed recaps of the real brawls they'd been in, were purely delightful: all the crashing and banging, and the blows of a contact sport, with nobody getting hurt and lots of heavy-drinking camaraderie afterwards, which was yet another kind of happy violence. There was also some high-speed horse-and-buggy work. My father actually leapt from a galloping horse to almost the top of a stagecoach, because Pendergrass had told an assistant director that he could. When he couldn't hold on, and fell off in a cloud of dust, it was hailed as perhaps the greatest scene in the movie. He didn't break any bones, but was so bruised and sore he quit and went back to San Francisco to look for a real job. My mother was working as an assistant librarian in the San Francisco College of Mortuary Science.

Somehow he fell in with a bunch of car and motorcycle racers and found he loved it. He was still wary of people getting in his face, but racing seemed almost to work as an anti-intrusive. His deep thoughts got even deeper and weirdly clearer the crazier the daredevilry. But the guys he ended up hanging around with were stupid and mean. Pendergrass had been accepted in a kind of proto-film school at USC, in the theater department, but had come back to kill time until the term began, and charmed everybody into the idea that he could make a racing movie. He had the run of the gang because he knew how to use them and was mean enough to do it. My father couldn't stand them. But every time one of them did something and gave him that lazy mean macho look, you know, suck my dick, you faggot lawyer, laying a southern accent, whether real or made-up, on thick, mah dog'd kill yo dog in a fight, he felt he absolutely had to show them that he could beat them—at whatever it was they were doing. He took, for instance, boxing lessons, so he could actually knock the fuckers down if he wanted to. But in the end, he was just addicted to being crazier than they were. One fight, he knocked the asshole down, and kicked him in the head. Another guy pulled him away and asked him why he kicked the man not only when he was down but in the fucking head, and my father said because he's a shit-sucking pinhead and I hate shit-sucking pinheads, that's why. I read that as: I have staved off suicidal depression by knocking an asshole unconscious: what's wrong with that?

There was one guy who had some business savvy, and he thought a lawyer might come in handy. He answered to just about any nickname that was offered: Barky, Buzz, Buddy, Burrito. My father never knew what his real name was. But they were down racing midgets and sprints and motorcycles and what have you—soap box derby specials, tricycles with rubber bands— around the Moffett Air Force base in Mountain View and Sunnyvale, where a man named Bill France the Younger was stationed. His Big Daddy was busy back east locking down Daytona as *his* race, *his* town, and he's sanctioning this and that, sanctioning his asshole and every turd that comes out of it and anything else that moves—he's got a telescope and the shit-house door wide-open—he's taking the race off the sand and A1A onto a banked concrete super-speedway that he himself is building, while Barky the fucking Burrito establishes the National Association of Stock Car Auto Racing on the West Coast and invites my father to be a stakeholder in the Daytona project.

My mother thinks this is childish bullshit, worse even than the childish bullshit of Hollywood movies, and they begin to have alcohol-fueled fights and weeping détentes. They talk about how beaten-down they are by the greater bullshit that is overwhelming the nation. The high spirits at the end of the world war, the gushing joy of being alive after a horrifying struggle with evil, the blithe moral superiority, were now being stamped into molds. Everybody was to think the same thoughts, talk the same talk, act out the new rituals of devotion to the infinite ascent of what was called the quality of life. They are living in a furnished apartment in the Mission, on Bryant Street, and when one day they realize that they've smashed up most of the landlady's plates and glasses, and that the landlady is sick and tired of their shouting, they swear off alcohol.

Then my mother gets a job at Pepperdine, a small, immensely wealthy Christian college in Malibu, for which she must dissemble a fundamentalist faith she believed she had outgrown. In fact, it turned out to be rather a reassembly of that faith. But it's happening almost without her knowledge, beneath the surface of a young woman who very much just wants to have fun, go to big, wild parties and dance, recite poetry while smoking cigarettes in a very long holder—not to dreary college evenings, where her colleagues seem suspicious, even dismissive of the secret workings of the brain. She wonders why they even have a psychology department, as they dare each other to make mom-and-pop jokes about Freud, or country folk fishing with cane poles and bobbers on the shore of Jung's collective unconscious, or Otto Rank, who said that the facts of life were best learned in the gutter, where sex was not controlled by God as a pleasant means of reproduction, and not an experience of the beautiful ecstasy of the true union of loving souls, but something that was plainly dirty, a thing inextricably linked to urine and feces. Alfred Kinsey's best-selling reports—males in 1948 and now females in '53—of what people actually told him about their sex lives, was derided as a mix of zoology and perversion and shoddy hearsay social science. The hundreds of thousands of people who were reading it. In the department office, a cartoon from *The New Yorker* was tacked to a bulletin board, showing two women examining the book. One says to the other, "Goodness! Is there a *Mrs.* Kinsey??" Especially naughty fun was had with Wilhelm Reich's orgasmatron, his orgone-energy collecting box, which people sat in for some kind of relief of whatever ailed them. My mother tried to point out that the box was an unfortunately silly conclusion to research that was actually quite strong and original.

This was, as I reconstruct it, one of a series of meetings of my mother and the devil at the crossroads. I don't mean that in that way the legendary bluesman Robert Johnson made a Faustian deal with the devil in the cotton fields of the delta, although my mother did indeed come to characterize those years as struggles with Satan.

For instance: her defense of Reich as a strong and original thinker was countered not with more scorn, but with a frank discussion about the actual value of strong and original work. Such work might be valuable in the long run and the big picture, but it was precisely *not her job* to teach it. She was to teach her students the fundamentals of the way the individual mind reconciled itself to others, in the service—this was most important—in the service of the princes of the state, who were in turn servants of the Almighty.

This called to something very deep in my mother's own psyche. She was, as any real thinker or artist is, absolutely committed to strong and original work, and she did not want to be primly appropriate about it. Despite her attraction to rebels without a cause, to the wild ones, to the ones on the road, to the free-living outskirts of Hollywood, *to her husband*, she wanted to reconcile those forces with the institutions of representative democracy, because they seemed good and sound to her. Terrible things were happening in the country, but it was a good country.

When my father admitted during the nightly drunken argument that he had kicked a man in the head, my mother started slapping him and wailing. She would never in a million years understand how he could have done such a thing, how he could have seen he'd come to such a thing and not turned away in horror. He began to weep too, and swore he would never do such a thing again. Something had just come over him. He wanted to believe it had never happened.

Another example: the stadium-evangelist Billy Graham came to Pepperdine to talk about his work. He denounced Kinsey and his work as the work of the devil. He said that the moral life of the country was in a steep decline. We were not climbing the narrow and rocky path to the Shining City on the Hill, but tumbling head-over-heels into the luridly lit swamps of Sodom and Gomorrah.

My mother stood and asked him a question at the end of his sermon-lecture. She wondered if it wasn't rather the case that Kinsey was describing life as it was actually being lived, and wouldn't that necessarily be helpful to

Christian reformers. Wasn't careful honesty preferable to polite repression? Graham's answer was that it was recklessly titillating even as it insisted it was soberly open-minded. The open mind was powerless against the evil winds of sin blowing through it like a door left open in a storm. The chaos of that tornado would soon destroy the home that might have withstood it if only Jesus Christ was the hearth of that poor dwelling, whose promise of eternal unconditional love was heat and light in the cold darkness of a world that was doomed. Polite conversations were the only way to advance ideas, especially when compared to the ranting and railing of atheists, communists, and degenerates—w

After he took a few more questions, Graham invited anyone who wanted to be born again in that universal love of Christ to come forward. People streamed down the aisles until it became clear that nearly everyone wanted to be born again.

My mother was one among who came forward. She wanted to live the life she was living, *and* live that life-in-Christ at the same time. She wanted to make them one life. She believed this was possible. That was what she wanted to study and write about, and that would be her life's work: the reconciliation of men and women as they were truly were with Christ as he truly was.

I have another connection to Billy Graham, and because my story is a history of my country as well, I will tell it here. The house I grew up in was the home of my aunt and uncle, my father's sister Darlene and her husband Alvin, who went by Okie. The house was on a small lake in Golden Valley, just off Golden Valley Road, a main thoroughfare that led to the frightening and forbidden "negro streets" (re: Ginsberg, in "Howl) of the North Side. On the other side of that road was one of the first houses to be built in Golden

Valley, a big mountain lodge of a place that had been built by Billy Graham's mentor, William Bell Riley. Riley was a friend of William Jennings Bryan, and was instrumental in getting Bryan to take on evolution in the Scopes Monkey Trial. Riley's second wife, who wrote his biography, was still living there when I was in high school. Her companion and housemaid used to come to our house with plates of cookies, things like Ting-a-Lings and ginger snaps with frosting, and Mrs. Riley herself used to invite us to dinner, as we did her. She died the year I graduated, and as she lay dying, Blanche, the companion, asked my uncle to come and talk to her. She was, apparently, hysterically afraid that demons had massed around her and were trying to drag her down to hell. My uncle, a good, kind man, tried to assure her that that was not the case, that Jesus's arms were firmly holding her in joyous being, and that she would soon be in Heaven, but she died gripped by the horror of another reality altogether.

The irony, of course, is that we perceived her from a reality in which demons did not exist, but of course they did, and for a moment, they were trying to drag her off to what was, for a moment, a consensual hell. She may or may not have existed in hell—but only for a moment, the moment itself an illusion of duration, of lapsing time, a service provided by the gods to help us measure the changing universe—. Until things changed again and heaven and hell no longer had the least bit of meaning. We were wrong to dismiss her terror as somehow not real, but right to reassure her. Our reality seemed so stable, and, frankly, unchanging, that hers stood out like a sore thumb. Yang and Yin, whom we now see as arch-enemy and noble protector, respectively, had the upper hand with her. Maybe she saw them, maybe she didn't. I'm just guessing. Just when I think I understand, I cease to understand. I hardly know who's speaking right now. There seems to be more than one of me at the podium. We are at odds. One telling a story, another offering commentary. I don't know if this is similar to the love and hate that threaten to tear me apart every day and every night.

Back to Malibu.

Pendergrass gets a job as a dialogue coach for actors trying to sound like gangsters or cowboys or cops or lawyers, and begins also to help the screenwriters with scenes that don't seem to be going anywhere. His suggestions tend toward the blowing up of a character's pretenses, the slapping off of a public mask and the revelation of some potent animus. Characters will break off their conversation and see, or rather hear, a car-crash off-stage. They return to their conversation changed by this violence. He begins to write whole scenes and is quickly hired to write episodes for TV westerns. My father begins to do legal work for this production or that. Pendergrass moves from his Quonset hut to a ramshackle cottage on the beach, in what was called the Colony in the 30s, where other young industry bohemians live in a drug-crazed splendor that has no relation whatsoever to the American Dream as it is being marketed. My parents move into the Quonset hut. They begin to drink again, and to smoke marijuana, and take Benzedrine in the morning and Seconal at night. They would get on the wagon, fall off the wagon, get back on the wagon, all the while trying to make the craziness meaningful, the endurance of it valuable as they find the good of it, and tried to find a way for that value to be recognized in the mainstream conformism of American life in the 50s. The Godly Work of the fabled Senator Joseph McCarthy of the great state of Wisconsin is burning its way through Hollywood, and his good Republican enablers are helping him destroy the Constitution because, you know, FDR was such a tyrant and they have been, you know, so long out of power, and the bad Republicans, the John Birchers and the garden variety paranoiacs are coming out of the woodwork. I am one year in the future.

"Did you yourself ever see Super Yin and Super Yang in those days, Daddy? I mean, when you were growing up and your parents were being so crazy?"

"Never once, my little sugar bunny. Things seemed to be as they were. Nothing ever seemed to change."

"But something happened next, right? What happened next?"

"Daddy has no plot, Judy," said Ann. "Infinite causes and conditions precipitate what seems like stasis."

"It wasn't until I started teaching creative writing that I began to see the violently repressive forces of the enemies of the open society at work, and to understand the constant struggle against it. I saw the evil in the good and the good in the evil. I saw Yin and Yang struggling not against each other but against the totalitarianism of the creativity profiteers."

In which Fred, who has been making his way to San Luis el Brujo in a wheelchair, joins the Yin group. His actions during the Crisis of 2008-2009 are reviewed.

14

Hauling on pulley ropes and swearing and singing like sailors, George and Judy haul Fred, who has been following them up the coast in his slightly slower wheelchair, up to the highest reaches of the tree house, which is nestled in a two-hundred-foot-tall *Pinus radiata*, aka in Ann's patois, Radiant Penis, aka Monterey Pine. He is still wearing the ripped and dirty orange t-shirt and blue tie. He has a five o'clock shadow the color of charcoal. He is inert, somnolent, frail. Ann is dressed like Sor Juana—black coif, white tunic, black scapular, golden beads brushing the floor—and George's hair is now bright orange. Judy, whose hair is white blonde with a pony-tail high on the back of her head, is dressed like and has the air of a think-tank policy wonk. Yin appears as well, in her white suit and helmet and sad old face.

"Moving forward," says Judy, twirling a pen between her fingers, "we should begin our conversation by asking each other what we want to see in terms of possible, probable, desirable outcomes."

Fred comes suddenly to life, making everybody jump. He intones grandly: "Where you are worth nothing, there you should want nothing."

George brings his hands together in prayer, and closes his eyes. "He speaks a sacred text of Samuel Beckett. In direct violation of Big Greeting Card's copyright."

"Moving forward," Judy repeats briskly, "any description

of future needs must be driven by recognition of how things stand right now."

"There has been," says Andie Bell, "a catastrophic loss of assets."

Fred thunders: "For I had one hundred and thirty thousand sheep, and of these I separated seven thousand for the clothing of orphans and widows and of needy and sick ones."

"What the man says," says Yin, "is nothing more and nothing less than the plain and simple truth."

"I had a herd of eight hundred dogs who watched my sheep and besides these, two hundred to watch my house. And I had nine mills working for the whole city and ships to carry goods, and I sent them into every city and into the villages to the feeble and sick and to those that were unfortunate."

"Fred's charitable giving," says Andie Bell, "is well documented. There are literally hundreds of foundation heads who will attest to his generosity."

They look down, down, down to the ground, where, like sunflowers, those heads have sprouted, demanding water.

"And I had three hundred and forty thousand asses, and of these I set aside five hundred, and the offspring of these I ordered to be sold, and the proceeds to be given to the poor and the needy. From all the lands the poor came to meet me!"

"The testimony goes on in this vein for quite a long time," murmurs Judy.

"Then everything was taken from me. Family, wealth, health—everything." Fred works on his phone for a moment, then plays a conversation he had recently with his children, Fred the Fifth and his twin sister Frederica, who are in their early twenties.

"Look, Dad," says Five, "Mom says we aren't your children."

"Of course you're my children! What—what are you saying? What are you talking about? That's insane! I love you more than anything else in the world! Did your mother—"

"No, Dad, listen," says Frederica. "Mom means you aren't our biological father."

"But you look just like me!"

"So does our biological dad."

"Dad, look, we love you, too, but we have to look out for ourselves here. I'm sure you understand that. We stand to lose an awful lot."

"I watched it all happen," says Yin. "Powerless to halt the relentless slaughter of well-being."

"Do you all remember Enron?" asks Andie Bell. "Of course not. The Enron gang were the 'smartest guys in the room,' right? 'America's Most Innovative Energy Company.' Well, surprise, surprise, they were just ordinary crooks. They went to prison and they cost their shareholders $74 billion."

"I happen to know, or knew, as they're dead, several of those shareholders," says Yin.

"So do I," says Fred. "By our friends you shall know us."

"It's a figure," says Andie Bell, "which pales in comparison to what happened just a few years later. Judy, do you have the figure?"

"Americans lost an estimated $12.8 trillion in the 2008 global financial meltdown."

"I know, knew, hundreds of those Americans in Hollywood alone," sighs Yin.

"The question of course is: did Fred lose all his money in 2008? Was he taking increasingly desperate gambles? Cooking his books just a little here and there until an avalanche killed him?"

"No, he was not!" shouts Yin angrily.

"No," agrees Andie Bell. "Indeed he was not."

"Just the opposite!" Yin goes on. "He saved the asses of those who their books did cook who their lives did gamble away!"

"It's not Job we should be thinking of here. It's Shakespeare's *Timon of Athens*," says Andie.

"'I am Misanthropos and hate mankind!'" announces Fred.

"The ultra-wealthy Athenian lord," George explains to Judy, "who was too generous to his friends—friends who refused to return the favor when Timon needed help."

"I actually love mankind," says Fred. "I want to produce a movie about a different Timon."

"Freddie gave and gave and gave," says Yin, "until there was nothing left to give."

"Yes. But. And this is important. Despite the fervency of your affirmations, I have to confess I cooked books—maybe not as innovatively as the smartest guys in the room, but certainly to the tune of some staggering fines—and made investments with not much more than desperation as my guide. The old good money after bad strategy that never fails. Plus, cocaine."

"So what we want," says Judy, "moving forward, is food and shelter for Freddie?"

Fred struggles back into the wheelchair.

"Health care," says Yin, to which everybody loudly assents.

"MO'BAMACARE!" hollered Judy. "Jeez, imagine if they'd called it Bible and Flag Care!"

"You will get your ragged and ridiculous ass out of that wheelchair permanently, Freddie! Mark my words. Mark my words." Yin is adamant, her dark face glowing fiercely.

"Of course you can stay with us," says George. "We'll pay for everything. We'll adopt you, send you to a good school."

"And you'll get a producer credit," says Ann.

"I appreciate the offers of help, but I'm really fine. I'll be totally okay on my own. In a way, I think I can say I've never felt better. I am more and more in tune with oneness."

"ONENESS!" shouts Yin.

"Oh, Yin, I mean the oneness of constant change."

"Well, okay then…." mopes Yin.

"What we don't understand," says Andie Bell, "at all, are the forces behind the video of the bike accident, and the dumping of leaflets all over town."

"'Fearless Freddie Funston the Fourth is a Fucking Fraud.' I love it. I totally love it. Don't you love it? You gotta love it."

"Whatever you are, Fred," says Ann, "you are not a fraud."

"Oh, we're all frauds, Ann. Come on. Constantly telling ourselves and whoever else will listen stories about ourselves, afraid to stop because we know we will disappear."

Ann surprises everybody: "Did you really like it when I chained and whipped you?"

"Honestly, no. I endured it because I loved you."

"Well, that's weird."

"I have to tell myself a story just to get out of bed," says George.

"What in the world have you got to be depressed about?" demands Ann.

"No reason."

"Moving forward," says Judy, interrupting her parents, "there are some questions we can ask ourselves."

"Is that the same as telling ourselves stories?" asks Ann. "Kind of interviewing ourselves with softballs?"

"*No, Mother.* I mean practical questions about what's happened to Freddie."

Andie Bell and Judy begin a fast pedagogical back-and-forth.

A: "Did Fred give away a lot of money to friends?
J: "Yes."
A: "Can those friends be looked to as resources?"
J: "No."
A: "Did Fred loan a lot of money?"
J: "Yes."
A: "Did Fred seek to recover some of those funds?"
J: "Yes."
A: "Did he employ private investigators and lawyers?"
J: "Yes."
A: "Were these people successful?"
J: "No."
A: "What was left in the wake of these attempts?"
J: "Animosity, bitterness, rancor, resentment."
A: "Is it not something of a paradox in human nature that benefactors invite hatred as often as gratitude for their good works?"
J: "It is."
A: "Was Fred truly kind?"
J: "Here is the rub, here is the nub."

"Or was he," interrupts George, "as Samuel Johnson described Lord Timon, a man whose ostentatious liberality scattered bounty but conferred no benefits, and bought flattery but no friendship?"

"He was," says Judy.

"Who said," George demands, "'O you gods! What a number of men eats Timon, and he sees them not! It grieves me to see so many dip their meat in one man's blood, and all the madness is, he cheers them up, too!'"

"Apemantus," cries Ann, "the Socratic/Diogenistic philosopher who weeps like Herakleitos at the apocalyptic folly of men who do not understand the Logos."

"PIETY AND FEAR!" orates Fred in mock-wrath. "RELIGION TO THE GODS, PEACE, JUSTICE, TRUTH, DOMESTIC AWE, NIGHT-REST, AND NEIGHBORHOOD! INSTRUCTION, MANNERS! MYSTERIES AND TRADES! DEGREES, OBSERVANCES, CUSTOMS, LAWS! DECLINE TO YOUR CONFOUNDING CONTRARIETIES! AND LET CONFUSION LIVE!"

"What are the smartest guys in the room plotting now?" Andie Bell continues.

"They are plotting the destruction of liberal democracy," answers Judy, "of the open society and 'small is beautiful' capitalism."

"What is the connection," asks Andie, "between the death of Student Z's father in the bike race, and her presence in George's class?"

J: "When she enrolled in the class, there was no connection."

A: "When was the connection made?"

J: "When it came into being."

A: "Is the past anything but brain residue?"

J: "No."

A: "Is the future anything but residue reorganized?"

J: "No."

A: "Memory to prediction to memory: is that reality?"

J: "Yes."

A: "Memory and prediction. Good and bad, hot and cold, wet and dry, night and day, birth and death. Is there any other logos?"

J: "No."

"YOU ERR!" shouts Super Yin.

"We do?" ask Andie and Judy simultaneously and in harmony, moving mezzo to agile coloratura.

"I am sick and tired of this table-tennis lifestyle! Yang does this, I do that. The only soundtrack is Harold Pinter's Ping Pong, *farse di insinuazioni violente*."

"I won't hear a word against Harold Pinter!" shouts George. "He saved my life when I was scooping turds out of the sink in the executive bathroom! I would have jumped off the Washington Avenue Bridge onto the John Berryman Memorial Splatter if it wasn't for Pinter and Beckett and Churchill, and, and, and Auggie Doggie and Doggie Daddy!"

"Who?"

"Stringberry! August Stringberry, the Svenska Mad-Hatter, the Last of the Alchemists!"

"When I get the upper hand in this opera buffa," growls Yin, "as I most certainly will, I am not going to give it up."

This gives everyone pause.

"Don't be silly. You have to" says Ann. "Otherwise you're no better *or different* than Yang."

"Fire is to everything as everything is to fire," moans Yin.

"Here she goes," says Fred.

"Fire is to the cosmic currency as gold is to human currency!"

"I'm too tired for philosophy, Yin," says Ann, suddenly listless. "I feel sick and weak. I'm aging fast, I'm weakening, I'm slowing, I'm hardening. I am becoming like the earth that is welcoming me."

"Mom," says Judy.

"Yes, Ann," says George, "stop talking like that. You are in your prime."

"No, Judy is in her prime. Andie Bell is in her prime. When I was born, W. Gamaliel Harding was President. My grandfather was the first governor of California. Your father is very much younger than I am, but you can't really say he's a spring chicken either."

"It's true," says Andie Bell. "I investigated. Both your mother's and your father's ancestors were extremely long-living, and spawned children, after an average of a century of abstinence, on their death beds."

15

In which the treehouse is bombed by the mysterious Piper Cub of Fred III seen in earlier chapters. Fred IV finds himself in two places at once. The Yin Group travels back in time to 1862 to see George's great-grandfather. Judy is torn between Andrea's trip to Manila to investigate Yang's partners, and the beginning of principal photography for A Heap of Gold in Minnesota.

They are standing behind a photographer, Adrian Ebell, at the edge of a plowed field near New Ulm, on the banks of the Minnesota River. But instead of seeing what Ebell is photographing, they are seeing a drive-in movie-screen-sized photograph appear, as if in a great developing tray. Ebell calls this photograph "People escaping from the Indian massacre of 1862 in Minnesota, at dinner on a prairie." He points to a little boy in the back, on his mother's lap, and tells them that the boy is one of George's great-grandparents, Sven Nestegaard. The image dissolves and they are back in the treehouse.

"Can we get back to fire," asks Fred.

"Fire," says Yin, "is a solvent. It provides Breakthrough Solutions willy nilly. Apologies, Freddie, for the reference to your ex." Strains of Willy Nilly's hit, "Ride Like the Mongol Horde" are heard for a moment.

"All right," says Judy, writing out a note in a mad scribble that seems to please her in its frenzied cogency, and which pleases the others, too, as witnesses to same.

"Is fire eternal and unchanging?" asks Yin.

"No," says Judy. "Yes?"

"The brain is always on fire. The 'clasping together' of the synaptical charge from neuron to neuron is more powerful than a lightning storm. The electrostatic potential of the latter is about three million volts per meter, and the former? Fourteen million volts per meter."

"The brain *is* fire," murmurs Judy.

"Yes," says Super Yin. "Intelligence is fire, the soul is fire. The universe is pure intelligence. But I must ask you again: is fire eternal and unchanging?"

"I don't know."

"It is not. Everything changes. The universe becomes, is, ceases to be. What does the universe become when it changes?"

"I don't know."

"Again: What is the greatest of the binary opposites?"

"The real and the unreal?"

"The real and the unreal. And what is the truth that lies beneath the appearances of the opposites?"

"I don't know, Super Yin."

"That they are the same thing. I'm saying Yang may indeed defeat me in this universe."

A small plane appears on the horizon, rising up from the sea. It seems to be heading straight for them. Judy dashes up to the observatory and trains the small refractor on the plane.

Then down she hurtles headlong, pale and trembling.

"It's…it's Fred. And an older man who looks just like him. With a moustache."

Fred struggles up from his wheelchair. George charges up the circular staircase, hauling on the handrails with such force that the structure trembles and creaks. Huffing and puffing and gulping and stumbling, he returns.

"It's that Piper Cub."

It is upon them, pulling up at the last second and banking steeply.

"There's no one in that plane," says Andie Bell.

"No," agrees Ann. "No one is flying the plane."

"But I saw Fred and….and Fred!" screams Judy.

"Either they parachuted out—" says George.

"We would have seen them!" shouts Ann.

Everyone but Fred scrambles up the staircase, which shudders and begins to come loose from the ceiling, and jam into the observatory just as the strafing Piper Cub covers the glass roof with so much shit—certainly more than the little plane is designed to carry—that the glass cracks under its weight. They watch the nearly liquid manure seep through the cracks, as if it is alls to pieces.

"What," asks Yin, picking shards of glass dripping with shit from Judy's hair, "is the opposite of gold?"

"I get it," says Judy through clenched teeth, tears mixing with shit in tracks down her lovely face.

"And what is true of all binary opposites?"

"I TOLD YOU I GET IT!"

George, who has managed to protect the telescope, steps away from it, slips and falls in some shit making a big splatting squirting sound, and says, "It was me in that plane."

Everyone makes subtle gestures or assumes slightly modified postures that clearly indicated interrogatory disbelief.

"Was I here the whole time?" asks George.

Affirmations of the most delicately tentative sort.

"No one looked up and wondered where I was at any time?"

Confused negations wandering to and fro the pales of observable consensual reality.

"Then it couldn't have been me."

Relieved adamancy.

"Right, Yin?"

The Creative Writers

"Nothing more real than the imagination," shrugs Yin.

"I don't know how to fly," says George. "Do I?"

After they all hose off, they inspect the tree house, and conclude that so much shit has fallen on it that it is structurally compromised. They kill and eat another emu, Ann finally admitting that she holds flightless birds in deepest contempt. Andie Bell ignites her scooter and says, "Well. I don't have any idea how this all is going to play out, but I'm going to Manila to root out the enemies of the open society."

Judy, who has rallied magnificently, says she will join Andie Bell.

"We are going," Ann demurs, "to start principal photography in Minnesota in less than a month."

"Judy?" asks Andie Bell.

"I'm committed to the film, but Mom, can't I get away for a few days?"

"So young and wearing so many hats!"

"On the one hand it's the story of my son's life—sorry, my father's life. I am committed to that truth. On the other hand, I am equally committed to all aspects of the truth, far beyond what our movie can accommodate, especially those that involve our fallen hero and friend, Fearless Freddie Funston the Fourth. And his friend Harry Mo'bama, who was once the President of the United States. At the end of the day I am dedicated to Popper and Schumacher, to *The Open Society* and *Small is Beautiful.*"

"I made *Gravity's Rainbow*, don't forget," says Fred. "You'd be surprised at how much a movie can accommodate."

"Look, I'll be honest," says George, "I thought I'd never want to see Olongapo again. But a part of me does. I know it's now weirdly, prohibitively expensive to shoot there—"

"We've found a slum in Florida that will do," says Ann.

"—*but maybe I want to shoot there anyway,*" he concludes, a little testily.

"They have a fake slum on a studio lot," Ann replies, testy as well, "if you're desperate for authenticity."

In which the Yin Group travels to Manila.

16

"Boarding for One World Airlines 101 to Manila is now closed."

They are all tucked into the metal tube, drinking champagne, spooning caviar into each other's mouths, ordering melting globes of chocolate, the surprise treats inside of which they have been assured will indeed surprise them. They are launched and become only a roaring in the heavens. The treats turn out to be deep-fried candied cat shit, extremely rare and available only on a black market where cats take in, it is estimated, trillions of dollars.

17

In which the Creative Writers solidify and extend their revolutionary control of the southwestern United States, enter into armed conflict with journalists, and host a visit from the 83rd reincarnation of the sublime Rhodo Don Dren.

The Creative Writers begin assigning ranks and regalia to all participants and facilitators. As a treat, everybody gets a glamorous makeover and headshot, as well as ready-made resumes featuring mission and vision statements complete with algorithmically-derived personal variations of the Five Magic Verbs: by far the most popular are Plan, Embrace, Improve, Empower, Fund. The top three trending Missions are:

1: to be Fair, Honest and Act with Integrity. We align our values, words and actions. We are honorable, trustworthy and sincere. We consistently go not just beyond the legal minimum to do what is right, but strive for the highest moral and ethical creativity.

2: to be Fiscally Responsible. We take seriously financial stability and our stewardship in carefully managing and constantly ensuring the best use of all public funds and other resources.

3: to be Excellent and Innovative, Amazing and Incredible. We aim to deliver the best service possible and measure quality outcomes and results. We strive to exceed expectations and to bring out the best in each other. We are flexible and adapt to the ever-changing needs of our community. We seek traditional as well as nontraditional solutions and embrace creativity. Core Values center on sustaining, developing, and advocating for creative writers and their work to realize their full artistic potential; fostering engagement towards an equitable, empathetic, and boundlessly imaginative world; witnessing the past, illuminating the present, and dreaming us forward. The work is grounded in the needs, desires, and sustainability of creative writers, and prioritizing long-term artistic relationships.

The Creative Writers lock up groups of Creative Workers for months at a time, for rigorous study sessions pointing toward acquisition of New Language of the People™, and require equal dedication to the service of the Community of Writers™. Duties include everything from manual labor in the pear orchards to sex on demand, aka spiritual communion in the heart of creativity, with the leadership—and only the leadership: celibacy is the rule otherwise, because while sexual activity masquerades as creativity in the biopsychological sense, it is an unstable, unpredictable pleasure that very quickly causes a collapse of discipline, and opens as well a portal for the demons of the earth to overcome weakened creatives. The Creative Workers are routinely sent on exhausting trips to other parts of Southern California, where, wearing an assortment of costumes from Big Fantasy's Gang of Five—*Star Trek, Star Wars, Lord of the Rings, Harry Potter,* and *Game of Thrones*—and playing ancient instruments to attract passersby, they sing rap-like propaganda in chanting monotones about the secrets of being happy and succeeding in life. (Another popular Mission is to Take Pleasure in the Work We Do. While maintaining a professional environment, we recognize the importance of building and maintaining an enjoyable workplace that will attract and retain quality employees. We value a sense of humor and remember not to take ourselves too seriously.) To make sure they're in step with Big Sloganeering, they form tight rank-and-file marching postures at regular intervals and shout that they are inclusive and diverse. When they are ignored or belittled, they are encouraged to become truculent and threatening, because quite a lot is at stake and people need to be shook and shook hard until they wake up: *Creative Writing is the only way, assholes. You can either get with the program now of your own free will and good sense, or you can be dragged into a re-education camp. One way or the other it's going to happen. In our spacious dormitories it's air-conditioned and you can watch sports. HEY ASSHOLE I'M TALKING TO YOU! In our re-education camps there's no air conditioning and you can't watch sports. OH YEAH? FUCK YOU TOO! Have you ever had creativity forced on you? It's a lot like having joy forced on you: not pretty. You feel joyless and stupid, until, like tortured dogs, you become helpless and begin to learn all over again YOU SHITSUCKING PINHEADS how to be a happy and successful creative writer, swaying and moaning and tidying up next to the angels in the Choir of Creatives in Heaven WHERE SAINT LEN OF BERNER MEETS YOU AT THE GATE AND EVERYBODY GETS SIX-FIGURE ADVANCES! Come on, people, don't make us mad at you! WE LOVE YOU!*

One day, a brawl breaks out between the Creative Writers and a small but heavily armed group rallying under a banner with these words from a Bruce Springsteen song: THE POETS DOWN HERE DON'T WRITE NOTHIN' AT ALL. THEY JUST STAND BACK AND LET IT ALL BE. A minimum-wage newsgatherer is clobbered over the head by a forty-year-old female Creative Writer and mother of two dressed as Captain Kirk. She is blasting BTS (her work focuses on the band) from a vintage boom-box, and uses it to render the foot-soldier of fake news unconscious.

Before she can dash the reporter's brains out, she is hustled off by the prominent Director of an MFA program, who has been brought in to manage security for the Community of Writers. When the reporter comes to, she sees someone sitting near her in the dark alleyway, someone clearly solicitous of her wellbeing, who wraps more ice in a towel and hands it to her. The kind stranger says that the Creative Writers know who she is, despite the many transformations she's undergone, from Faculty Adviser for the student newspaper, to Guest Essayist for the *New York Times*, to hand-to-mouth beat-reporter.

"They're tying up loose ends," says the stranger. "You'd be dead if Master Tobias hadn't intervened remotely. They want you scared, not dead, apparently. But this is an act of desperation, not strength. They've been selling millions of copies of Zhdanov's *Remarks to Soviet Writers* repackaged as *Cheerful and Profound Entertainment for the People*, and millions more of Mao's *Talks at the Yenan Forum on Literature and Art* repackaged as *Creative Writing is Good for All the People*, and I'm sure I won't surprise you much by saying a purge is taking place. Non-creative and untruthful writers are being arrested, tortured, tried, and executed for articles and speeches they've made suggesting creativity is not a religion. There's more I'd like to tell you, if you're willing to listen."

The least of it is news that a rogue AI tactical squad has developed portable smart-wombs, which allow anybody to get pregnant. Hailed as a Breakthrough Solution for gender equity, their first big order comes from the Community of Writers™. Advancement in the Community has always depended on indoctrinating new member-customer-workers, and with Big Publishing signaling they are ready for mass production, the Community makes it illegal not to bear as many Creative Writers as is practically feasible. And: to soften their image after too many brawls and suspicious deaths, they are bringing in His Holy Celebratedness, the 83rd Rhodo Dron Den to burnish their Spiritual Entrepreneurship global street cred.

Orgí and Alice puzzle over translated contract documents from the Chinese government, who believe they own and operate His Celebratedness.

"'Thank you for your service,'" murmurs Alice. She reads, back and forth from papers to phone. "'Party of the first part…herein…hereafter as…open brackets, Act of God whose resistance we reject, close brackets…as often and as long as parties enter awareness…either case…such as to give pleasure on one hand or on the other to give pain…grants and assigns full term…blah drivel blah snort wheedle… exclusive rights…mandatory reincarnation…*mandatory reincarnation?*'"

"From communist China, I know!" cries Orgí.

"'…costs against any sums…remedies for failure to reincarnate—What the fuck is that supposed to mean? Chinese power ballads…net receipts…index prepared by third party…the Field of Truth and Battlefield of Life… climbing the heights of yoga…interweaving of the forces of Nature…even as the unwise work selfishly in the bondage of selfish works…the unselfish goodwill of a billion Chinese persons…desire and wrath born of passionate desire…the great evil…the sum and substance of imagination…total destruction…hate and lust and yadda yadda yadda.'"

"Chinese power ballads?" wonders Orgí wanly.

"Hmm, I… *Diànyuán mínyáo*…that's what, a sales clerk's folksong? Oh, I think it's yes, the so-called Powerful Three at the top of Chinese political hierarchies, westernized as guitar, bass, and drums in the service of the music of the people…?"

"I assumed," says Orgí sadly, "that it was basically a promise not to kidnap His Celebratedness. Non-enforcement of extradition rights specific to a treaty the specific features of which escape me?"

"But we don't have an extradition treaty with China."

"Yes," answers Orgí angrily. "Something else is…being alluded to. And I'm just really irritated with this mandatory reincarnation business!"

Alice riffles through a big stack of files. "Ah. Here we go. 'The Walleye Llama speculated earlier this year that he might not reincarnate, thus ending his spiritual lineage. China, keen to engineer a process that produces a pro-Beijing monk as the spiritual leader of Tibetans, reacted angrily to that suggestion, insisting that the officially atheist Chinese government was the only one with the authority to make that decision.' I guess that goes for all Tibetan lineages, including his Celebratedness."

"Still: this is such good news, don't you think?" murmurs Orgí moodily.

"We have to install a new toilet for him."

"Why?"

"Doesn't say."

"Well then I want a new toilet, too, goddammit."

"Oh come on."

"Don't tell me to come on!" shouts Orgí sassily.

"You've got a whole wing for your personal hygiene."

"I want the kind of toilet that one of the world's greatest spiritual entrepreneurs has got."

"Well, I like to crap outdoors. I've dedicated a hundred acres for it."

"And by the way, are you as sick as I am of pretending to give a shit what the AWP thinks?"

"Oh my goodness yes. Bureaucrats is the nicest thing I can say."

"I say we crush them. Start swallowing up as many outlying programs as we can. Tobias, the wintry Master of the East, has made good progress, but the time to strike is now, while we've got momentum."

"Agreed."

"Now, before it's too late."

"Too late? Too late for what?"

"Wake up for Christ's sake! Market share is fluid and unstable!"

Alice sighs and waves in acquiescence, returns to the contract. She peers squinting at it, and whispers to herself. What has appeared to be a window with a view of spruce- and snow-covered mountains, changes. It is a color wheel now.

"It's easy to make fun of gurus. But it's just as easy to make fun of astrophysicists with their gigantic blackboards of equations. Astrophysicists don't comfort people who are frightened and suffering and exhausted. If you mix opposites on the color wheel, look at this for minute, will you? And stop complaining? You get a black that feels black, as opposed to actual black that just seems like a hole in the painting. You get what they call in high frequency trading a 'dark pool.' We want the dark pool everywhere people look when His Celebratedness arrives. They must be inviting, alluring, seductive, just as we ourselves are. But. The dark pools must be merely veils over actual black holes, cosmic black holes, but of course microscopic. I think we can do this. I really do. We'll be able to suck in anybody who looks at a dark pool before they know what's hit 'em. Which of course is an all-expenses-paid trip to the Heart of Creation, with us as Spiritual Guides."

The screen changes to blue light, then orange light, then a dark pool.

The Creative Writers

In the campus auditorium, the President of the Student Body addresses conference attendees.

"I am so honored to be here, my fellow boys and girls. As president of this great institution, this community of writers fiercely dedicated to compassionate learning and making the world a better place to be, I can say that this is one of the greatest and most important days of my life. We are here to grant the title of Honorary Doctor of Humane Letters and I will repeat that because they are big and important words: Honorary Doctor of Humane Letters to His Celebratedness, the 83rd Rhodo Dron Den."

Pause for standing ovation.

"He will occupy a newly endowed chair, The Ronald Reagan Chair of Poverty, Plague, Famine, and War."

Pause for another standing ovation.

"This Chair was named after a little boy—"

And another standing ovation.

"—who turned out to be the greatest gift to creativity this great nation of ours has ever known."

An unprecedented fourth standing ovation.

"Ronald Ray-Gun knew that only the Enemies of Creativity™ were opposed to the formation of the Titanic Monopolies of Entertainment™, and only Darn Fools™ would balk at making the kind of money that came of Massive Overhead™ and Increased Profit-Margins™, and only Supercilious Elites™ would criticize the empowering union of creative writing programs and young adult literature."

This standing ovation goes on for hours.

"And now, here he is, ladies and gentlemen, the one and only His Celebratedness, the 83rd Rhodo Dron Den, who will offer us glorious words of wisdom that have been handed down to him over the course of millennia. Mr. Rhododendron? Sorry: *Dron Den*. Ha! Sorry. Your

Celebratedness? Oh: turn off your cellphones, etc., and be civil. Pardon me, Your uh Rhodododo…dodoness. I'm sorry, please go ahead."

The standing ovation is replaced by the kind of screaming that only the Beatles used to command.

Rhodo Don Dren is dressed in black tights. Even his face is clothed in this way. On the top of his head is a little white mask, human but featureless. He keeps his head bowed most of the time, so the little mask is all the audience sees, with the rest of him swallowed up in an oversized and overstuffed armchair. He mumbles to his sidekick, a dog, who translates and holds the mic in his mouth at the same time.

"I am often asked if I am the Buddha. I find it hard to believe people ask me such things. The answer is easy: no."

Standing ovation.

"No, please do not stand and ovate. It will take much too long. I have nothing to say and it would be wrong to take a lot of time to not say it."

Pause for standing o that doesn't happen.

"Good. I am also asked many questions that the Buddha answered thousands of years ago, as if these questions and answers were not available on the Internet. Please excuse my incivility: there is nothing in my contract that stipulates I be anything but human."

Standing ovation.

"No, no, no. Now what did I just say? The Buddha found questions quite tiresome, too, I assure you. History suggests he was good at not desiring an end to tiresome questions. I am not so good. I would say that 'I try to not desire an end to tiresome questions,' but that would not be true. Some of you have heard that you should kill the Buddha if you see him on the road. Is that road rage? I'm sorry, there is much that I am not familiar with in the United

States of America. But killing the Buddha is a good idea, as far as I can see. Some of you have heard that you should burn all practices, and that, too, is a good idea. But try to not make a religion out of burning all practices. Simply stop. Another question: what is the self? I do not know. My friend and I have a little conversational fun with the Four Ways That One Can Say I Do Not Know. But this is not the place for that. As to the self, I can say only that for all intents and purposes you are nothing without it. Ha ha, that is a joke, but it is also true. The self is an illusion but without it you would be nothing. Being nothing is not all it's been cracked up to be. It is not so bad. In fact it is quite good. In truth there is no other way to be, willy-nilly. Is that right? 'Willy-nilly'? Whether you will or no? Free will is a masturbation fantasy. I ask you to tell me who you are. Are you your self? Very good: find this self for me. Are your self and your body the same thing? If I chop off your arms and legs, are you still you? If I pluck out your eyes and stop up your ears and sew your mouth shut: still you? Replace your organs with artificial machines? Still you? Are you you when you are asleep? Are you you in a coma? In a persistent vegetative state for decades? Is the self in the brain, no matter what kind of shape it's in? Where in the brain? In this electrified three pounds of pudding, where are you? If your brain stops, is that the end of the self? And where and how did your brain begin? Were you in there somewhere from the beginning? Before the beginning? After the end? So much illusion. Enjoy your illusion. If you can. If you cannot, then you must think a bit further. Your brain, wherever it came from, whenever it started to be yours—ah ha! The brain is yours? But I thought the brain was you! No? You own it? Fine. Caveat emptor. Your brain can only tell you what has already happened. Based upon what has happened, it insists it can predict what will happen. There is that word again: will. You say you chose to come here tonight. And that you will go home when I have finished speaking. But think of the infinitude of causes and conditions that came together in that moment that allowed you to decide to come here! And think of the infinitude of effects and conditions that will have come together when you do arrive at your home. Do not live enslaved to this elusive illusion, this self who says there was a yesterday and will be a tomorrow. Past and future collide in this thing we call the present, this thing we call now, but which is the illusion of illusions! This collision of past and future never happened because past and future do not exist and the now cannot be found! When you have found the self, show me the now. You are scientists! Do so, please! Find these things and show them to me! You may think you can but that is nothing more than the illusory self making up thoughts to entertain itself. And only itself! If you overhear people talking, you pay as little attention as you can, but if they should happen to mention your name…! Ha! What then? The self jumps upright! Yes, it is like an erection! It wants to be stroked and squeezed with all the news these other selves have to tell it! Yes, very selfish indeed is the self. My self, my thoughts, my life, my money, my erection, my will to orgasm. The self worries and plots and weeps and rehearses, yes, rehearses the past and the future in the hope that it will be able to shout from the rooftops that it does indeed have free will, autonomy, security! But no. Even if the self gets what it wants, it will want something else. It will change its mind, and you who are watching yourself will feel helpless, hoping for the best, desiring pleasure, fearing pain, wondering from where you have come and to where you are going. You are going nowhere! Here is everywhere, now is eternity. Do not let the miserable scheming tyrant self keep you from enjoying this illusion. We know nothing about it but we cannot deny that we are seeing it, hearing it, tasting and feeling and smelling it. That miserable self will bar you with miserably entertaining thoughts that close the door on the day and bar it utterly! You will be alone in a room like so many of Samuel Beckett's characters. This wonderfully learned European playwright: did you know that he is a champion of non-duality? Of ancient *advaita*, of the not-two? That mouth shouting from a hole in the curtain for fifteen minutes about the terror and misery she endures? Yes. His Nemesis was Descartes."

Unrest in the audience. Nobody knows who Descartes is.

"The Nemesis of our Descartes is Descartes, too. Did you not know that?"

Unrest, some shouts. Nobody wants to know who Descartes is.

"Good night. Do not get up. Do not applaud. I have said nothing, given you nothing. Go home, if you can, and marvel at the infinitude of causes and conditions impinging on your journey. Yes. And when you come home, you will see it is a different home and you will marvel at it, just as you will marvel at the you that is different, now that the self has been reduced to quaint murmuring and puffs of smoke and you can see that St. Francis was right: what you are looking for is what is looking. There, I've finished, and just in time, as I see the gendarmes pulling open the great doors of the gate of this *sanctum spectacularis*. Ah, the jig, *mes amis*, is up! I raped a pretty little nun with a prickly-soft shaved head, and gave her three-quarters of a million dollars to go away with the child, whom she insists on thinking will be the reincarnation of My Celebratedness—*even though I'm still alive*, right? And keep quiet, but sadly, it was not enough, and she has not kept quiet. The child's people have begun a campaign to convince the world He is Me. I will not contest this, as the proof is overwhelming. He *is* Me. I will go to prison and think about what I have done and what it might mean for the next Me. Maybe I'll die quickly and my whatever will flow into my child with such force that the delay won't matter. Goodnight, everybody! You've been a great audience!"

A great hue and cry is raised and loosed in the Palais de la *créativité*. There are many stroboscopic color explosions, as if this is after all just part of the show. Then: BLACKOUT! The Creative Writers tear around the place in voluble dismay. They will have to hire Crisis Managers and somehow make this development seem an example of what…the chaos that underlies creativity? That they and only they know how to tame and make socially useful and spiritually virtuous? And just exactly on whose authority is Rhodo Dron Den being arrested? Our authority is nothing to sneeze at! This seems doable, very doable, the more they think about it. The faith of most of the creative writers in them would not be shaken if they were asked to sacrifice themselves for the greater good. Instead of a disaster, this could be a *coup de foudre* that smashes everything that stands in their way. They've already got a hot Intellectual Properties law firm at their beck and call, as it proved necessary to formally own everything the creative workers wrote, and the firm's sub-specialty, golf and tennis law, has helped them get quickly into the teeming and sordid sports dollar market where the original goal was simply to dominate the Chinese entertainment market, but which might now be modified to the point where the Department of State will have no choice but to give them a nuclear football. Might they not just set up an independent state for His Holy Celebratedness, along the lines, say, of the Vatican? They just might!

18

In which a visit to Olongapo shocks George with economic changes. They travel to Sulawesi. Ann sickens and is unable to fly. They confront the Neanderthal Marvin the Martian.

The naval base commissioned by Fred the First's Commander in Chief, Teddy Roosevelt, which had seen a million sailors and soldiers a year come and go during the Vietnam War, was no more, leaving in its place a clean and quiet suburb of Olongapo called Subic Bay Freeport. No more as well Shit River, the drainage canal where warriors of the Greatest Country on Earth amused themselves by tossing nickels and dimes into the sewage and poor and starving children dove for them.

"What did you do, Daddy," asks Judy, "in the war?"

"Made little boys and girls eat shit."

"At least you didn't murder them," says Fred. "At least you didn't drive your bayonet into the belly of a pregnant teenager."

They let themselves be dazzled by the clear and sparkling water, refreshed by the cool and dry air.

"We mustered here before going into town to walk around."

They cross Magsaysay Bridge. But what George remembers as an expanse of slum on the edge of mountainous jungle, is now a chic district of quiet tea and coffee shops, temperature and humidity-controlled bookshops, small performing spaces where talking-gong and gamelan music is played. Green and blue Moluccan parrots speak a half-dozen languages enjoy small plates of delicate vegetables and sweet fruits. The memory of the little girl cut nearly in half by razor-sharp buckles in an errant swing during a belt-fight—that and all memories of himself as a sailor, as a gunner's mate and shore-patrolman, a soldier of empire, are no more than vestiges of a metempsychotic other life.

But he wants desperately to remember, to remember well, finely, accurately, truthfully. He wants to understand how he has come to this moment, to understand the chaos and clockwork of the universe and his place in it.

Ann's wings have receded into her shoulder blades and spine. She can't draw them out. She does not understand what is happening to her. Her back and neck and the base of her skull feel as if it's all a piece of concrete, and she wants to leave.

Yet she, too, desperately wants to remember, to reconcile the past with the present and the present with the future. How did she come to have wings? But for some reason, Yang's dark stasis seems to be working on her more quickly than the others. It's difficult to know anything, to learn and unlearn the real and the unreal, to get to the bottom of it, where the so-called unreal is seen as part of the real, as real as everything else in the universe.

George insists they go to Sulawesi, to Maros in the south of the island, thinking that some prehistoric cave-tourism will restore her sense of balance, then off they'd go to Bali, but Ann is afraid, afraid like she has not been since she was a little girl with no wings. She has been sick before, to be sure, deathly ill more than once, and her wings had seemed burdens, but this is different. George is either oblivious in the ordinary way men often are, or knows something about what is happening that she does not. They agree to go.

Just as the motorized scooter was the epitome of

highspeed travel in Southern California, here the obvious choice is a triple-hulled dugout with bamboo outriggers and a hempen sail dyed bright red with a golden wing on it.

They paddle easily, almost languidly, meditatively, through the gray and purple and silver and turquoise waters of the Celebes Sea, and down the Makassar Strait, passing the stately island cities of the great container ships, their fashionable arts districts lit in charming yellows and greens, colors that almost magically ward off depression and anxiety.

Up the Sungai Jeneberang, they drift past immense tamarind trees, their fruit pods like homunculi in cocoons, or like tiny, baby-mummies hung instead of buried, and the soaring columnar faces of the limestone mountains, with their long noses, deep-set eyes, cracked and crooked mouths and dripping green beards.

And then, the hallucinogenic dreaminess deepening, they are in the cave, the mind of the cave, the cave of the mind. Their pupils dilate, their hearts beat faster, then slower, then faster again. George and Judy share a Mars bar: George believes he has already eaten it sometime in the distant past, while Judy believes it's something she is going to do in the distant future—and yet it is clear that the Mars bar was there for a moment in front of them, then gone. They can still taste it. Fred levitates an inch or two from his wheelchair, settles, rises up again and settles again, and begins a sitting dance characterized mainly by stomping and moaning while he rolls himself around and around the circle of their campfire until he begins to hallucinate, calling out to and conversing with family ghosts. Ann's wings explode from her shoulder blades with the sound of a thousand grouse fleeing a copse. But they are covered in a kind of fluid, a thick transparent glue that suggests an amnion. She thinks she might be dying.

There is her hand reaching out to the wall of the cave.

The Creative Writers

There is her flute, hoving into view and into her mouth. There is the spit, the piss, the ochre and charcoal dust, the vegetable juice and albumen blowing out the end of it, spattering around her hand. There is her tiny daughter, waving her stick of boar bristle, a babirusa appearing on the wall. There is her immensely old husband, bent double but lunging up and down, drawing an incomprehensible set of figures: an array of red stars flowing as if around a bend in the river, a ladder, a gently round-edged triangle, and a self-portrait of the artist, contemplation of which causes her to giggle.

She takes him to be a species of Martian, à la Loony Tunes and Bugs Bunny: Marvin the Martian, that's his name, almost all head, and the head almost all eye, crowned by some kind of curious headgear, and what she takes to be a gigantic propeller or wind-up mechanism attached to the base of the skull. Three tongues shoot from its mouth. One leg is stretched out before it, the other cocked beneath it, à la the men of R. Crumb's "Keep On Truckin'" comics. It is an exact duplicate, or rather, an original that looks exactly like another original in La Pasiega in northern Spain. Both have been conclusively dated—but wait! She realizes that the painting in Spain is 64,000 years old, and this one is 44,000 years old. 20,000 years of art had produced an identical copy.

When the painter steps away from his painting, and his shadow on the cave wall becomes much larger, he is no longer old, but also no longer human—no longer *sapiens*, he corrects her: *neanderthalis*. His legs are too short and his torso too big a barrel. His brow slopes and his chin disappears. His occipital bun is, however, magnificent.

He says, twisting a little stick in the hole of another stick in a bed of dried grass and wood shavings, "The universe is composed of notes and instruments to play the notes acted on by violent inexorable forces: change this way, change that way. One crucial hand rises up out of the maelstrom, one flailing arm brushing the warm sandy beach at just the moment past and future approach and stare lovingly at each other, and you know what our genus has known for millions of carefully marked and measured years, that calm is often shoulder to shoulder in the yoke with the panic of something slipping entirely out of control, and that there appear to be two worlds: one within the brain and the other without. It seems to be the case that the world without swirls with the force of a hurricane into the world within, and utterly destroys it in an eternal present, destroys it so completely and continuously that it seems untouched. A kind of an eye of the storm settles over the brain. In Truth there is no eye and there is no storm. The exploding sun and the ordinarily functioning brain are one in the same. Only a devoted anti-solipsist would imagine there is anything like a boundary to be marked or a distinction to be made. But here there is a breakdown of the instruments of individual perception. Human senses are insufficient to the task and the world takes on the character of a violent assault on the *solus ipse*, which mounts a counter assault. Pleasant sensations and painful sensations alike are processed by lightning. Living appears to be—appears to be—the overwhelming of one thing by another, one storm by another storm spawning a new storm. The universe appears to function only in violent collision. This is however only an illusion. It is an illusion generated by the mind that the mind knows to be false. The mind knows it is false and generates a second force whose only object is creation—not violent creation, but creation that is expressly not violent, the creations of the imagination made material via horse-hair, burnt bones, lime, clay, cave water, vegetable juice, animal fat, blood, marrow, albumen, urine and rust, the art of the Gondwanalanders."

This is the incantation necessary for the recovery of Ann's health. This is the speech that is latent in everything George has ever said to her. This is the ur-text of their mythic marriage.

Her wings grow and grow and become very much larger than her body, ten times the size of her body. One is green and the other is golden. The green wing brushes Fred and he falls in convulsions to the floor of the cave. The golden wing brushes him and he relaxes. After a moment he rolls over and pushes up on hands and knees. Then he stands, unsteadily to be sure, but burning oxygen in magnificent gales of elemental force.

Ann whispers to George: "*Homo* is not meant to fly. My wings are ten times as powerful as they were. They are capable of great good and great evil. The stronger my wings, the less human I am."

Marriages founded on power imbalance are doomed to be unhappy. They do not succeed. Yin and Yang—not incarnate, not intellectual, but as true as gravity—redouble their efforts, feeling angry and thwarted. Every last illusion of control slips away. Fire judges and condemns all.

Her green wing lies across the campfire. It begins to smolder. Panicking, she stumbles from the cave, striking her head hard against a jutting piece of a tremendous stalagmite, formed so intricately it looks like a temple in Angkor Wat, but is an artifact of a civilization far older than that.

The green wing is smoking now, and, as she leaps from the cave and rises up—massive wings beating thunderously, thin plumes of smoke barely visible in the gray sky trailing from it— it catches fire. Soon the gold wing is aflame as well. She dives into the place where the Java and Banda Seas meet, and swims for a hundred miles, sizzling wings leaving boiled seawater in their wakes, to Bali, where she hopes to catch a puppet show or some *legong* child-dancing, but where she finds herself instead in the middle of the Hindu New Year celebration of silence. And she thinks, as she dries and warms herself, of Thoreau: *the falling dew seems to strain and purify the air and I am soothed with an infinite stillness… Vast hollows of silence stretch away on every side, and my being expands in proportion, and fills them. Now can I appreciate sound, and find it musical.*

In which a meeting with the Thunderbird takes place in southwestern Minnesota. Judy has a fateful call with Andrea, who has uncovered metastasizing evil in the funding of Gravity's Rainbow.

19

Just a few miles east of the narrow road to the deep north, US Highway 71, in southwestern Minnesota, and just a few miles north of what had once been the Joutsen farm, George, Ann, Judy, and Fred—who is walking now with a cane—are examining the Jeffers petroglyphs. These are shallow relief carvings in an outcropping of billion-year-old red and pink quartzite that stretches south to Iowa and north to Brown County, where the famous Browns Valley Man had been dug up and judged to be as old as Glacial Lake Agassiz. It is early winter and the prairie grasses that grow up in the cracks of the bedrock are withered, but no snow has fallen. The corn and bean fields are desolate with ragged stalks and plundered earth. No birds sing, and the wind is cold and buffeting. They are entranced by the carving of Thunderbird. With its triangular body and angular, naked-line wings, it is nothing like the Birdman of Lascaux, the stick-figure with the little bird-cap, bird-baton, and scimitar-like erection, and yet it is clearly the same creature, just as the thousand hands are carvings from quartzite and not paintings on limestone as they'd been in Sulawesi, or Chauvet, but are the same hands after all, separated merely by ten thousand or twenty thousand or forty thousand years.

At some point after they've absorbed the wind and become cold itself, and the silence become heavenly, the ground begins to tremble. Californians, they recognize it immediately as an earthquake. But in the space between the closing and opening of their eyes, Thunderbird has raised itself and shaken out its immense dark wings. *I control*, it seemed to say, *the rain and create thunder with my wings. I fight those creatures who hate mankind and live under the water. I punish moral depravity.*

"We," says Ann, flourishing without arrogance her own wings, "are moral warriors who know that there is no difference between a heap of gold and a pile of shit."

In reply to which Thunderbird seems to say people cannot fly.

"Oh yes we can."

"You will pay a price for it."

"Happy to, you cryptozoological teratorn."

"You will not be happy."

"I assure you I will be."

"You will not succeed."

"Want to bet?"

"Your husband is a sage and speaks wisdom."

"I am?" George can't help but blushing blurt. "I do?"

"He wears the lapis lazuli pants, the shamrock green belt, the white tunic of the gods, and his hair is the color of a burning orange. He speaks of the prison of thought. Silence is our true nature. The voices in your head that insist you are ghosts. They no longer exist and yet you nurture them. The mind is a graveyard. There is nothing more real and consequently more deadly than the imagination. How can you be happy when the future is always the past?"

"Democrats," says Andie Bell, leaning confidentially over her phone, sitting with a cup of coffee at a table all but lost in a sea of travelers at Chek Lap Kok airport, "lost more than one thousand seats in state legislatures, governors' mansions, and Congress during Harry's time in office. It was a slow-motion landslide. He was advised to spend almost two trillion to jump-start the economy but went with Larry Summers and a much lower figure so he could work on healthcare."

"Mo'bamacare!" shouts Judy, sitting on the bed in an old-fashioned motor hotel in New Ulm. "Wasn't Larry Summers the president of Harvard?"

"Yes."

"Andie Bell, seriously, what do you think my chances are of getting into Harvard Law?"

"I have no idea, Judy. Why do you want to?"

"I want to hang out with the decision-makers of tomorrow, and be their conscience. You know, curate their fortunes, advise them in meditation sessions that both tranquilize and inspire."

"This is not well-known, but our new President went to law school in Iowa."

"Rob Sand went to law school in Iowa?"

"He wanted to remain Governor, and never leave his friends and family in Iowa, but the Presidency is an offer you can't refuse. The Ivy League is scrambling to give him honorary doctorates. But there are so many of those on the market now that the price is just about to go through the floor."

"Wow. Okay."

"What I want you to think about now is this: what happens when a powerful man fails to play the game well?"

"Andie Bell, I don't know. How could I know that?"

"He leaves the door wide open to unscrupulous persons who do play the game well. By cheating. A little bit here and a little bit there, or globally. Did you know that many people who are acknowledged to be great players are in fact only great cheaters? And that nobody cares so long as you are great? Unless you are caught? At which point nobody cares how great you were because all you are now is a scumbag?"

"I did not know that, and it's ideal-crushing to think it's so."

"I want you to think about who actually wins in a given political deal that seems on the surface to be the fruit of good progressive policy. Oh dear, they're calling my flight."

"I don't know, Andie Bell. Who benefits?"

"Think about how expendable professors have become, how they have been steadily replaced by gig employee adjuncts, and how the cost of tuition is skyrocketing. Where's all that money going? Remember: Student Super Z paid $50,000 and was taught by your father, who made $3,000. Where's all that money going?"

"The mafia?"

"Yes. Organized Crime. The forces of Super Yang. People who want to be seen as playing the game fairly but who above all do not want to be cut out of the action."

"Is that…is that what Freddie was doing?"

"It might be. Familiarize yourself with a man nicknamed Low Tech Joe. That name celebrates his real name, Low Taek Jho, aka Jho Low, because he is an old-fashioned money launderer and briber who likes to wear disguises and who scorns the algorithms and data analytics of the younger criminals. He also likes to hang out with celebrities. He gave Kim Kardashian a Ferrari and Leonardo DiCaprio a Braque and a Picasso. He gave John Gleason Yang, aka Super Yang, the Heaps of Gold Museum, which doubles as his office, in which you were nearly born. His home has a golden pyramid in its garden. He and two other bankers, Roger Ng and Timothy Leissner, of Goldman Sachs, were responsible for a three-part, six-billion-dollar bond scheme: Project Magnolia, Project Maximus, and Project Catalye. Low Tech Joe is at large and has been seen in Phuket, Macau, Hong

Kong, Taiwan, Shanghai, and Manila—the latter being the last place anybody thought he'd turn up. He's probably had face-altering surgery, maybe even more than once, and he bankrolled *Gravity's Rainbow*."

"Oh dear."

"Did Freddie have anything to do with the schemes? Absolutely not. Is he caught up in it anyway? Absolutely yes. Okay, last call to board. Gotta go. We know there is big crime at the top, and we know that as well with the Young Republicans, the Bikers for the Right or whatever they were called, Z's father and uncle and who knows who else. We have to find out who was flying the Piper Cub and why they were dumping anti-Freddie leaflets. Gotta go, gotta go. Love to everybody."

20

In which a re-enactment of the Dakota War of 1862 opens a door to other realms of being.

Behind the motel, on the edge of a cornfield, one phase of the Dakota War of 1862 is being re-enacted by tribespeople from the Lake Traverse Reservation and members of the New Ulm Historical Society. Smoke pours from several well-established residences, some two stories tall, and fire is consuming another large home. Little Crow, who had gone to Washington, D.C. a few years earlier and gotten fucked in the ass, has acquiesced to the rage of a small number of young men who have already killed some Germans while stealing eggs. A remark of the government trader Andrew Jackson Myrick rings in their ears: "So far as I am concerned, if they are hungry let them eat grass or their own dung." In this re-enactment, Little Crow rides a white horse and is aiming a Winchester rifle. Wahpeton and Sisseton warriors are wearing leggings only. Some have feathers tied in their hair. Women and children and infants lie slaughtered at their feet, blood seeping into the dirt and grass, causing Fred to compare the words of General Jake the Juggernaut of the Philippines to whatever commands Little Crow may or may not have uttered.

All these actors have become statues. Earth and sky are Turneresque swirls of feverishly pigmented light. Bodies are enameled and lacquered. Only their eyes are alive. As George takes closer note of these eyes, and Fred whispers how the

The Creative Writers

corpses of Filipino women and children are stacking up on the corpses of Minnesotan women and children, he finally begins to question the nature of the reality he is experiencing. What exactly is a re-enactment, after all?

"Where is your great-grandfather, Dad?" Judy asks.

"He's in a hastily built stockade in Belmont Township, Jackson County, which became Fort Belmont, near which my grandmother and mother were born. In a few months he will watch the biggest mass execution in U.S. History—biggest even after Abe Lincoln trimmed the number of executees from three hundred and three to thirty-eight. Everybody involved, Judy, think about this, everybody involved only wanted to be happy and successful in life."

"Well, yeah, but I guess at some point you have to check yourself, right? And ask yourself if you're really going to be happy killing babies."

"Judy, does it seem strange to you that your mother can fly and that I look like a cartoon character?"

"Not really, no. You put it like that and of course it sounds a little odd, but no, I don't think it's 'strange.'"

"I have been thinking about how I sometimes stop and wonder if I'm…if I'm not dreaming in the usual sense, which would be silly, but incontrovertibly asleep and dreaming that I am incontrovertibly asleep and dreaming that all I have to do is wake up to get me out of this pickle: where did I park my car, or what the address is where I'm supposed to meet someone, or why my parents hate me, or why I have to carry so much stuff from place to place. You know?"

"Not really…? I dream about dying and then standing by your bed crying and asking how you could fail to see that I'm on fire."

Judy is enveloped in pale flames that are roaring in a vortex from one of the burning houses.

"I mean look at the eyes of these statues. Do they look live to you? I have this terrible feeling in my guts that these Dakota boys are going to come to life and kill us all. Do they look like that to you?"

Judy merely crackles.

George dreams of his mother and father. They are both gibbering mad and flailing away at him. While this is certainly embarrassing and annoying, he can't understand why he has harbored such hostility toward them. They are both clearly insane and could in no way have provided him a stable, loving home. Which he got from his aunt and uncle anyway. After the debauchery of Malibu, his mother got a job teaching in Hong Kong, and his father a job with the State Department in Paris. They placed him in a reputable boarding school run by the Lutheran Brethren for wealthy and powerful Lutherans who subscribed heartily to Luther's belief that the princes of the realm must not only be obeyed but catered to and cultivated, because, obviously, no proper church could get by without kissing a little ass for the coughing-up of a little dough. It was near Fergus Falls, in the far north of Minnesota—also not far, cineastes, from Fargo, where the Coen Bros, Amos and Andy, built an entire company town like Ilya Khrzhanovsky did in Ukraine, paying people to live and work there, and be filmed over the course of a decade. The town was named Donnelly, after Ignatius Donnelly, though that man had never had the least connection to the town. His fifth-grade teacher, though, Mr. Donell Dale Tornell, had spent the better part of a cold, dreary morning telling them all about Donnelly, feeling that cranks and weirdos had as much to do with American history as some run of the mill founding father. Donnelly had founded an eutopia near what is now

Hastings-on-the-Mississippi with money from friends in Philadelphia, one of whom gave the town its name, Nininger. This was just before the Civil War, and the Panic of 1857 did them in, making the place a true utopia, *id est*, a nowhere. Donnelly nevertheless became a U.S. Congressman, and then Lieutenant Governor, and wrote many bestselling books, about Atlantis, most notably, which he seems almost to have invented himself but which now of course has solid consensus affirming its fantastical existence and ruin, and another about Francis Bacon being Shakespeare—which of course we know is wrong, but close, with Elizabeth I emerging and now the uncontested author of the all the plays except *Hamlet*, which was written by Hamlet himself, because who could write such a story but the man who had lived it, right? Dictating the final scene as he lay dying? You just could *not* make that stuff up. Once the Grand Inquisitors of 21st Century Literature set us all straight, the conclusion could not have been clearer.

And that in any case was where George lived until he was eleven and moved to the Sweeny Lake District in the Minneapolis suburb of Silver Valley. His mother, Lorraine, left Hong Kong and quickly became an expert in religious schizophrenia, even as her own became troublesome. Marrying again, to an influential player in the Military-Religious Complex (flagandbible.com) in San Diego, she became world famous for living the life she wrote about. Her TED-talk, "Why You Have To Be A Little Crazy To Love Jesus," was known to anybody who knew what a TED-talk was. She was credited, in fact, with putting TED-talks on the map. When George joined the Navy, he was stationed for a while in San Diego, telling everybody he knew that the place had once been described by Gore Vidal as "the Vatican of the John Birch Society." Nobody had the least idea what he was talking about, and this pleased him greatly. He lived in Imperial Beach with a view of the German Expressionist-style barbed-wire fence surrounding The Helicopter Capital of the World. It was a trashy little house in which thousands of young men had been allowed to vomit in peace—in his case to the soothing rhythms of *A White Sportcoat and a Pink Crustacean*, an album of Caribbean-Country-Folk-Rock that introduced him, via liner notes, to the novels of Thomas McGuane. The drive between Imperial Beach and La Jolla was like being carried in a Terry Gilliam dream through a tunnel made of billboards of Nixon's gigantic face, the deep blue shadow of a beard over the jowls, the bushy eyebrows, the hunched shoulders and the arms straight up flashing Vs for victory, and the words I AM A CROOK! THAT'S WHY YOU LOVE ME! Visits were often dull and difficult in the ordinary ways, but just as often resulted in hysteria, with Mom going for him with slaps and shrieks, which made his move to the South China Sea one of great relief.

In the dream, he became more and more certain that he was about to come to a great discovery, not just about who his parents were, and who, by extension, he was, but of what was called human consciousness and—had he gotten this right?--low-entropy universe? It was moments like that that convinced him he was dreaming, only for his certitude to be swallowed up in centuries-long discussions around a fire in a cave at the tip of South Africa with Super Yin and Super Yang. These superheroes, or independent contractors, or slaves, or whatever they truly were, seemed peaceful and mysterious, as if they had slipped from their earthly costumes without his knowing. He asked them if they had manifested to, say, Ignatius Donnelly, as they had to him. What had his parents known of them? Superheroes hadn't really existed in their day, had they? Why was there no trace of them in history, in dinner-table conversation?

The dream darkened. He feared he was being confronted with hallucinations on the brink of substantiality, that just as matter was energy constrained, the hallucinations were becoming material via the force of his thought. This choking, paralyzing fear lasted a very long time—until he realized it was playing out just like an ordinary horror movie, and began laughing at it. Very quickly, however, this cheap giggling bored him, and the dream became one of frustration and growing anxiety that it wouldn't ever end. Yin and Yang swirled around each other, and asked him what he saw.

"Featureless, eternal, omnipresent gray," he replied.

"This is how we have been perceived by most . We appear in black and white only at moments of birth and death. And of course in TV shows, movies, celebrity bios, and so on, which is why our talent agency avatars are so busy. When Reagan commenced his brutal war on regulation , when they began to fear and hate the other nine thousand nine-hundred and ninety-nine things…ah, poor soul, this was when the Great Crisis began to shake the foundations of the human and the real."

"Forgive my ignorance, O my masters!" George cried out.

"We arose in your world, O George Joutsen, because the creative writers, who perceived you as their enemy, those very people who were once your colleagues, have set themselves on a path that leads directly and with terrible swiftness to the heat-death of the universe. They look to yang as their champion, but he is so only in the world of appearances, just as yin is your champion: only until it is not. But look, you're missing the point of this dream, and that is to understand and grasp and act upon the gifts your parents bequeathed to you."

As he begins to wake up to the usual hypnopompic hallucinations—a farmer in ripped overalls standing in the doorway, an AM radio voice doing local commercials and commodities prices, with faint noises suggestive of the rhythms of a baseball game announcer and crowd reacting to an exciting play—George wonders why the lives of his parents, despite their obvious struggles and failures, despite the pain and the misery, seemed so normal. Or perhaps the better way to put it was why his life, and his alone, did not, why his was so strange and adrift from the laws of the universe. Other people's children, for instance, appeared to take years to grow up, not days. Was it simply a matter of perception? That things seemed weird to everybody, privately, but not publicly? That the only obligation was to go with the flow? Everyone was at odds with reality, and constantly trying to fashion a new and better one, one more suited to…to what? The constraints of belief and the secret desires of one's own mind? Was the reason— here was an idea—that now he had real money? *Lots* of real money? No, it didn't add up— but what was he supposed to do about it? It had all started to go awry when he was fired by the Creative Writers. But why? And again: what was he supposed to do about it? Infinite causes and conditions had carried him along like a leaf in a river, past—here came another thought, somehow in quotes, then suddenly in huge block letters leaping out in deep relief from a stone wall— "ECSTASIES AND AGONIES! DELIRIUMS! BREAKDOWNS! DEMENTIAS!"—now in terrifying or exhilarating rapids, now slowly rotating in mucky backwaters, and the only way it was possible to *not* live the life that was being lived was to die. Perhaps he is only being given access to something other than ordinary consciousness, the sub- or unconscious, the greater part of who he is, but which he has never known.

21

In which principal photography for A Heap of Gold begins. Other realms of being interfere with the shooting. Student Z, now known as Super Z, begins a work of terrorism planned by Yang. The Earth of the Mind slips it mooring and reality is overwhelmed.

They are gathered, hundreds of them—because this is a major motion picture now—around a controlled intersection on a four-lane divided highway, just west of downtown Minneapolis. The crew is about to shoot the road rage fight that is central—hear him out—to both George's story of his father's murder and the feigned violence that exploded in his classroom, and how all that explains everything you need to know about the human condition. George and Judy are off to one side. Judy has a clipboard at which she peers closely and frequently but no obvious end. Her husband, a Dinka-Norwegian paragon named Henrik, just retired from a short but brilliant career as a basketball player, has his ear to Judy's hugely pregnant belly most of the time.

"So it was rush hour, eight in the morning. I'd been up all night. I merged from Highway 12 onto the Belt Line. Guy behind me pulls up really close and tailgates me for a minute. I see him leering and grimacing in my rear-view mirror. Then BANG he rams me! I'm instantly choking with rage, right? Who wouldn't be? But all I can think to do is try to read his license plate number backwards. He takes the next exit, onto this highway right here, ol' 55, the Floyd B. Olson Memorial Highway. Have I told you who Floyd B. Olson was?"

Judy, flipping pages on the clipboard, says, "Governor during the Depression?"

"Declared a moratorium on farm foreclosures in 1932. My grandfather was the last farmer in Jackson County to lose his farm. Also had close ties to the mob. Had a reporter killed. One takes the bad with good, I guess."

The actor playing George is George as he was just before he was fired. He is banging his fist on the window of the other car.

ACTOR: WHAT THE FUCK IS THE MATTER WITH YOU, YOU FUCKING ASSHOLE!

OTHER DRIVER pushes his door open and shoves ACTOR.

ANN floats down to them.

ANN: Cut. Let's do it again.

They do it again and again and again until it looks utterly ridiculous and everybody is laughing.

"So he takes the exit," George says to Judy and Henrik, "but because I'm in my beat-up but zippy little MGB, I swing in behind him. I'm telling myself all I want to do is get his license number. I get it...and we come to this stoplight here, Wirth Parkway. Which is red. And I say to myself, I can't just sit here and pretend it never happened. I'll ask him why he did it.

DRIVER hits ACTOR in the mouth.

ACTOR: That the best you can do, Chumley?

"Oh Dad," snickers Judy. "You didn't really say that, did you?"

"I did! I think I thought I was in a comic book or something. A movie. Action hero. Chumley: can't recall who I'm referring to. A cartoon walrus?"

Chumley the Cartoon Walrus strolls past and nods knowingly.

Henrik, in his delicately balanced African-Scandinavian sing-song, says "Arnold, Clint, Sylvester—yust like in your essay, Dod: men whoo can dodge boolets and make visecracks. The greatest Americans of yoo all."

ACTOR grabs DRIVER by the throat and backs him into the wedge of the car door and the body of the car, trapping his arms. DRIVER'S face gets red and his eyes bug out. ACTOR'S fist is cocked for a merciless beating—and then he seems to come to.

ACTOR: What am I doing?

"What was I doing?" George asks Judy and Henrik.

The light changes. Horns honk and traffic starts to pass them. ACTOR releases DRIVER'S throat and steps back. DRIVER takes this opportunity to lunge at ACTOR and launch a wild swing. ACTOR takes hold of DRIVER and throws him to the ground.

Screech of brakes. A big utilities truck runs over DRIVER.

"Wait, wait, wait," says George. "That's not how it happened. The truck swerved and missed him. What just happened? Ann! Ann! Hello? Ann? That's not how is happened!"

Everyone on the set seems terrified. The truck has skidded through the intersection. TRUCK DRIVER jumps from the cab and runs back to the crowd. Three or four more cars pile into each other.

ANN: Cut.

"Mom wanted to run the scene both ways, Dad. Did she not tell you? Guy gets killed, guy doesn't get killed. Didn't she tell you?"

"No."

"Are you okay, Dad?"

"No, I thought...I thought, no, something went wrong.

I thought the stuntmen...mistimed something. I thought the guy was dead. *For Christ's sake, I thought the guy was dead!*"

We see a black-and-white montage—technically, "a dazzling montage"—of images, ranging in tone from rich-and-creamy to lurid-and-grotesque: ambulance arriving at the scene of the accident, dead body splayed and splattered on highway, cops handcuffing George, cell door slamming, little man in white room, eye at peephole, courtroom with wildly gesticulating lawyers, grim judge, immense gavel (shuddering frame of reference as it's brought down), George on the filthy toilet in his cell, head in hands, pants around his ankles.

FADE TO BLACK.

INT. HOTEL ROOM - NIGHT

Ann and George are in bed, reading. Loud knocking at the door. George swears with brutal color and opens it. It's Judy. She's frightened.

"Honey what is it?" asks George, taking hold of her. "What's the matter?"

"Judy?" Ann calls out. "What's the matter, sweetie?"

"Flight 101. Andie Bell's plane. It's disappeared. Yang took it. Yin might have been with her."

FADE TO BLACK.

EXT. FARM - DAY AND NIGHT

We are seeing a farmhouse, barn, and outbuildings from a drone camera. We are hearing sonic booms in fast succession. Day changes to night to day to night, like a strobe light. Then everything slows and we see a car pull up to the farmhouse. SOLDIER, dressed in camo, gets out and goes to the door. FATHER appears. There is apparently a brief conversation, at the end of which they grapple with each other. SOLDIER pulls a gun and shoots FATHER. SOLDIER stumbles to his car and swerves crazily out to the dirt road and then almost in the ditch of the paved county road. He takes a left on Highway 71 and disappears into the wild green yonder.

The crew emerges from the outbuildings, and Ann settles to the ground, handing her camera to the AD and folding her wings. She walks over, musing, to George and Judy and Henrik, who are outside their trailer.

"So the United Nations," says George, "condemns it as a flagrant violation of international law, but there's broad popular support here because, well, Americans love killing, especially commies and black men. Desire for happiness and success put our hapless soldier on a hilltop in a Jeep with four other commandos. They had only a tourist map, and they were lost. They were then ambushed, and everybody but our man was killed. He came home messed up, was discharged, enrolled as a creative writer at the University of Northern Iowa, tried to kill himself two times, dropped out, and drove north on Highway 71 until he came to our farm, killed my father, wrote a poem about it, and killed himself."

They all turn as one to gaze at two stunt-doubles, who are wrestling on the porch. After a moment, George grabs Ann's arm.

"What the...is that Student Super Z?"

Ann stiffens. "Is it?"

Judy laughs at her parents. "Oh come on you two. She's really good at it."

"She's what?" George demands.

Super Yang climbs out of a limo that had just arrived in a cloud of night-dark dust. Ike Perlmutter and a hundred Private Equity Clowns tumble out of another, ready to deploy cognitive biases and give everybody around them the illusion of control while fleecing them good and proper.

"Okay, maybe you missed this," says Judy. "She was

actually in the Army. And trained as a boxer. Competed as a boxer. Went to Israel as part of some kind of goodwill sporting tournament, and fought the Israeli champ, who was twice her age."

"Israeli champ? Sharon Friedman?" sputters George.

"Yes, I think so."

"Sharon Friedman was my agent in the 90s!"

"Wow, Dad. Small world."

"I just heard about Yin and Andie Bell," says Yang, putting on a sad face. "Poor old Yin! Just got weaker and weaker, and jeepers, now there's no more Yin!"

"Oh you can't kill Yin, Yang, you puffed up pile of poop," says George, who nevertheless feels a deep, strange blackness infiltrating his optic nerves.

Z and the other stunt-double are wrestling for the gun.

Judy and Henrik, who are dressed as Elizabethans for unclear reasons, possibly to keep their father's imagination bubbling, adjust each other's costumes. Z steps away and fires the gun four times, striking and killing them both.

"No," says George. "No, no, no, NO! This is NOT how it's supposed to happen!"

"IT'S HOW IT'S HAPPENING, BABY!" roars Yang.

In the terrified clamor, Ann rises up and hovers in the air, shrieking.

The crew films her. This crew is in turn filmed by another crew. Around the film crew filming the film crew filming the scene, another crowd of people has formed. They seem merely to be watching as the action unfolds, unmoved, but intent. Student Super Z slips away, then returns. Everyone, in all the crews and crowds, stops and stares at her.

I could be watching a crew filming a scene of fake violence," thinks George, *when suddenly real violence breaks out. Or the real violence could just be an extension of the fake violence, exponentially more fake. I could be in a dream, unable to wake up, or I could simply be having a dream about having a dream about—*

"'Let one thing be certain!'" shouts Z, "'You shall all have your grand death! The Earth is clamoring for victims, and we shall see a splendid massacre!'"

George recognizes this as a line from Jean-Claude Carrière's script for Peter Brook's *The Mahabharata*. He had seen the nine-hour play in a quarry outside Avignon in 1985, traveling on a grant from the Jerome Foundation. Thirty years later it was a required text in his class. So Z must *not* have been sleeping all the time! She must have learned something from him! In the violent incoherence of his immediate environment, this knowledge strikes him as a blast of satisfaction flowing from a job well done.

The drugged quality that often overcomes victims of terror passes through the crowd. Eyes close, some people fall to their knees in either terrified supplication or cataplexy. Super Yang flashes here and there among them like a woodland fairy, screaming frightening laughter. Some people watch the catastrophe on a screen, and are in turn watched by people in the dark. Others simply stare at the thing itself—not an idea about the thing or a representation of the thing, but the thing

Z reveals her suicide vest.

"Matter changes," she whispers telepathically to her erstwhile teacher. "The heap of gold and the pile of shit are one."

"That's not an excuse," George whispers back, "to kill people."

"Oh yes it is."

"No, please, no."

Ann descends from the fog in which she has been

temporarily shrouded, into the great and magnificent lights of the movie set. She shrieks, and her talons are out. There is an explosion, followed by a blinding light that completely overwhelms the lesser lights. The shockwaves are not the kind that cool heroes can surf.

22

In which the discoherent real slowly begins to cohere once again, affording George one last talk with his mother and father about the nature of the real and its primal field.

At some point in the not-time that follows, in the stinking, mysterious vapor of the not-space, George comes across a long letter from his father. Unable to read it in the weird glare, he folds the ten pages of miniscule but perfectly clear black-ink script into his pocket. It begins to seep through the thin cloth of the pocket, along the unraveling seams, and be absorbed into his flesh. It flows in his bloodstream like an antibody searching for disease-bearing bacteria—or something else entirely. The idea that he must somehow come to understand who his parents were, and learn from them, throbs like a heart in a distant part of his body.

"Dear George Junior," he wrote. "Language is an awkward and laughably self-important means of transport from essence to essence, from—here's a perfect illustration—*mind to mind*, but it's all we've got and what're we gonna do about it? Just for starters, dear unknowable stranger, you who leapt into being when I erupted in a tremendous shower of sperm into the echo chamber of your mad mother's incubator of silk and steel: what is a mind and what is moving from one to another? But no, no, no: I must take hold. This is a just a letter to tell you I am leaving Sarcelles in *les banlieues* of Paris because the French are so tiresome and offensive as they dish out the frank speech and prove unable to take it. Maybe I'm just a slow-burning Midwesterner after all: slow burn, the fuse impervious to the assault on its life (a life precious to itself, as all life is?), and the inevitable explosion. Your mother must have told you about the time I kicked W in the noggin. All I can tell you is that it wasn't a man that I knocked down, not really, and it wasn't a head I kicked, and the whole unseemly process turned out, I think, to be good for both of us: as we used to say in the Air Force when a plane crashed and everybody died in the flames, *lesson learned*. But here I am again, wanting very much to slap a few haughty judgmental faces. Do you have a bad temper? I hope not. Terrible way to live."

Dad, Dad, Dad, murmurs George with the breath and lips and tongue of someone sleeping on his face, *I threw a guy under a speeding truck once. I don't know if he lived or died. I guess it's like Billy Jack Carter said during his campaign, in that* Playboy . *I murdered a man in my heart.*

"Once you start slapping faces, it's hard to stop. It's an addiction and gives pleasure like all addictions, but is unsustainable, like all addictions, like all pleasures. That is why I resisted all notions of an armed left. *Soixante-huit* was exciting for many of us, for just that reason: *Je suis Marxiste—tendance Groucho*. Fascists must first and steadily be laughed at. I was in a group going around with Wilhelm Reich. Some were tossing his books at the cops, but we were hurling Reich himself. You may know that before your mother became a religious fanatic, she taught and wrote about Wilhelm Reich. Maybe you don't even know who he is. Student and colleague of Freud, wrote *The Mass Psychology of Fascism* in 1933 and *The Sexual Revolution* (I'm sure you know that phrase!) in 1936. This is no place for a recap (the purpose of this letter, however, is to tell you where that place is), but suffice it to say that while the family unit is not the source of fascism, it is the primary mechanism or molecule.

Fascism thrives on repression and guilt and shame and the violence that naturally comes from all that horror, and the so-called 'learned helplessness' as your mother and her crowd call it, 'stupidity' I call it, and I don't mean lunkheads, I mean people who have been stupefied by religion and pop-culture, who have been cowed (an insult to the animals I loved when I was a boy on the farm) into believing there's, on one hand, a hard and impenetrable barrier between good and evil, between us and them, and contradictorily, no barrier at all, requiring constant policing and punishment of thought and deed. But your mother, back to your mother. When the FBI came down hard on Reich and his Orgasmatron, which they believed was fraudulent, he disappeared and your mother wrote voluminously and persuasively on his behalf. Some people thought he was dead, some in hiding, some in prison. Hard to understand how he could have been living openly and happily in Paris, dining out regularly with renegades from the State Department like me…but no one said law and order was anything but a mystifying nightmare from which only hallucinogens can wake us. We put a spell on him that allowed us to drop him from as high as the fourth floor of a building, and be shot from a cannon, etc., and we did so during those glorious weeks in May when we chased Charles de Gaulle not just from office but from the country! Imagine that! Here's a word to the wise: de Gaulle and his fellow Catholic conservatives *had a monopoly on TV and radio*. That was normally understood as part of a propaganda effort, but they also controlled *le Surhomme* and *la Femme Merveilleuse*. I remember you writing to me, you must have been eight or ten, and your cousins had forced you to read *Harriet the Spy*, which you grudgingly admitted was a good book even for boys. But you were confused by the lesson Harriet learned, which was that sometimes you had to lie, and by Wonder Woman's lasso of truth. I wish I could remember what I told you. Probably nothing, as I was a terrible father. I flatter myself, or maybe I'm whistling past the graveyard of our relationship, that neither you nor I care about who we should have been to each other, for each other, because we have bigger fish to fry, or deeper fish—fish swimming more deeply in the sea of mind, I guess I must clarify, though who knows, maybe some fish are profound philosophers as well. I once pulled in a talking fish, but it was just inane blabbering small-talk, *yeah, I see what you're saying and no, you're right, the sister-in-law has a lot to answer for, a big fish is gonna eat a little fish and I don't see any way around that*, and I killed the carp-lipped pebble-head, and ate him instead of playing along. Anyhoo! The bigger fish I mean, and here we are finally to the point of this letter, is education that doesn't produce fascists."

"You're wrong," declares the mother in his blood, quiescent no longer. "Religion doesn't necessarily produce fascists. And you're just ignoring, willfully or not, the main properties and functions of belief."

"Here we go," says George Senior. "The family is the mechanism and religion is the fuel, Nadia. Any exceptions prove the rule. Now please stop. This is so tiresome, and this is my time with George anyway."

"Oh please: *your* time with George? Give me a break. I cannot bear it."

"WHO HAD TO SUDDENLY MOVE TO HONG KONG? IT WASN'T ME, NADIA!"

"I am just as much a part of his blood as you are—and by the way, George Junior, I hope it's clear to you that the father and mother we are here in your blood are not the mother and father you know outside your body. You don't really know us outside your body, but here, sweetheart, we know each other so well as to be one. I can't hurt you here, as I know I've done there. The slapping and the shrieking, I regret it all so much. Everything we say here is just a part of oxygenation. It's neither healthy nor unhealthy. It's just incontrovertibly part of what is. And what is, is continuous. Fourteen billion years and counting."

Mmther, fmther, no, murmurs George, still face down on his pillow, his arm over his head, the other trapped against his side and numb, *you did not hurt me. You confused me, but I am no longer confused. When my dogs died or were taken from me, I was hurt. Nothing else hurt me. Only children accuse their parents. I am a man.*

After this clash of chemicals in his blood, his father's letter continues its flow. But when had his father written the letter? It seems so long ago as to be an artifact of history—bearing no trace of the emotion, however faultily or clumsily expressed—that normally marks such family literature. Still on the verge of dream panic with his mouth and nose pressed, as in a murder, so heavily against the pillow, he wants to know what it looks like in Sarcelles, if in fact that was where he was, and how he made it through day after day working for a government he was so opposed to—because isn't that how people are driven mad? By the bondage of the desire to reconcile that irreconcilable? Or was it simply the desire that drove people mad? That was the grain of golden truth in everything the Buddhist flim-flam men perpetrated, wasn't it?

"I'm going to quote a friend of mine, George Junior, a historian named Chuckie Olson, whose work I hope you will read, and the sooner the better, because I want you to help me teach in my new school, and the following ideas are central, foundational: I wonder if that has any meaning for you. I take it to mean that most of life is invisible, and that what's invisible is what matters most. We know very little about what matters most, and most of us actually hold it in contempt. I see it this way: we enslave ourselves to the visible."

"I couldn't agree with you more," says Nadia, in a calm and friendly tone. Then up an octave and many decibels: "THAT'S WHERE RELIGION COMES IN!"

George's dream-father seems to nod politely at his dream-mother. He becomes her for a moment, and she him. Then they are one, elemental energy constrained in the shape of a wheel slowly rotating. George wonders at how terrible and sublime their victory over him would have been had they been united all along. He's glad he has money and power now, and can live as if he is singular and impregnably bound. I want, he thinks, to be dirty and sexy, swallowing gold doubloons, shitting them out, and rolling around in it while all the women in the world make love to me in a mass sexual event like the world has never seen before! Some of these women slowly gather around him. They are part of a circus. A trapeze artist—she has wings but is not Ann—flies him up to her perch. She flips upside down so that her cunt is pressing against his mouth. He washes his face in her lotions while they spin around the circumference of the great ring below them.

But who's that below them? The audience is standing up on their seats and reaching for them, shaking their fists and howling in outrage. Dear God. It's the Creative Writers and a regiment of Creative Workers. Out of the corner of his kaleidoscopic eye, spinning madly above them like a spy satellite: is that a sniper? *Why me?* he wails. *Why me?* Faster and faster and faster, but always seeing, in hideous clarity, the rifle, the glowing lens of the scope, the dark shape cradling it. I am too great to die, he thinks, in a kind of reflex, too great a spirit, and yes, okay, I could die, they might kill me, I see the bullet snug in its chamber, a spermatozoa of death, but my great spirit will live on and never let them rest in their wickedness and enjoy their revenues for a second.

His father has continued to speak, and has apparently been going on for some time. George has lost the context. He's just going to have to wing it, to make sense of what his father and possibly his mother have to say without any spoon-feeding or complaints that he doesn't understand or get the reference or whatever it is adult children say when the Enemies of the Creative Writers try to pull a fast one with a book that isn't about coming of age in fairyland, or seems to lack an appropriate social message. He listens to his father. Over and over again, he feels as he used to feel when he read a book and began to learn about the invisible world. He is mesmerized.

"It is sometimes said that a human being is like a wave rising up as it nears the shore. It feels singular. Its destiny is clear: to smash itself upon the rocks and sand, and so it does, believing that no other wave has achieved such greatness in its dark but translucent mystery of hydrogen and oxygen and awesome career…and lapses back into what it always was—nk Michaux, a painter and expert on the origins of Chinese ideograms (just as Chuckie the Cheese—that's a nickname, by the way, from his days as a pitcher on the Harvard squad—knows Mayan) sees it in a way he calls terrifying, as water constrained in a pipe by a faucet: when the valve is open, he lives, and when it closes, he dies. And please forgive, in light of these metaphors of water, my meandering discourse. Rather, don't forgive but try to understand, because this is central and foundational— yes, I see I am repeating myself—to learning and teaching: *the flow of knowledge of what is* and *language as pictures of ideas about things as they are.* I hope you see the difference between the head of the jaguar and the Mayan word for it: *bahlam*. Both Chuckie and Hank felt that there was an immediacy to ideograms that other written languages, e.g. cuneiform, lacked. And immediacy is all, George. Mediation of knowledge destroys it. It becomes bookkeeping for slave-owners. Mass mediation is mass destruction. Learning happens when the teacher and the student, however these entities are constituted, draw as near as they possibly can to the source of consciousness, of thought, to the vortex, as the poets used to say a handful of decades ago. Here (I was gone for a moment, looking for this) are the first lines of a poem, or essay, by Pound (whom you could have been reading instead of galivanting around the South China Sea as a hired gun for an international death squad): 'The vortex is the point of maximum energy. It represents, in mechanics, the greatest efficiency. We use the words "greatest efficiency" in the precise sense—as they would be used in a text book of MECHANICS. You may think of man as that toward which perception moves. You may think of him as the TOY of circumstance, as the plastic substance RECEIVING impressions. OR you may think of him as DIRECTING a certain fluid force against circumstance, as CONCEIVING instead of merely observing and reflecting.' If you draw near that perfectly black vortex, you will, as Hank has said, be privy to the tiniest shards and flakes and bubbles of perception. Back to Pound: the student/teacher will 'see the picture that means a hundred poems, the music that means a hundred pictures, the most highly energized statement, the statement that has not yet SPENT itself in expression, but which is the most capable of expressing.'"

This is when the dream begins to break up, or rather to attenuate and lengthen, becoming meaningless in a way opposite to the break-up mode, as if it were a transmission from the event horizon of a black hole. This, at least, is how he imagines it.

In the ensuing silence that grows between bits of data, he hears the unmistakable voices of the Creative Writers, most clearly and loudly—as usual, he chuckles to himself—that of Orgí Paráfora, with Alice Reznya providing an icily superior ground note, Billy Greggs and Harry Lorenzo tut-tutting like a pair of cartoon clarinets, all the while releasing intestinal gas they claim does not come from them and which doesn't smell anyway. He can make out one sentence before this transmission too breaks up: "The AI stuff we've been doing on hate speech and bullying classification proves there is no other way than an automatic way to solve these problems. There is no other way."

Oh for CHRIST'S SAKE, pleads George. *What is it NOW?*

His father's letter picks up where it left off.

"There is a field of energy that is the source of everything. For us, right now, for our particular purposes here, let's call it a field of thought."

George II can only describe this idea as *galvanizing*. Electric current, biochemical electricity, not quite strong enough to disable him, hums up and down the length of his addled body. He has long thought that he lives in a prison of thought, and senses now that George I feels as if he's been in prison all his life, too, but is out now, is free, and wants to know if they can be of service to each other. He hopes, for example, to find a way to employ me as a teacher—which is exactly what I want to do. So much of this nightmare of preposterously good fortune and bad fortune, these assaults on memory and imagination, this Destruction of the Temple—now wait, isn't that a sci-fi novel by Barry Malzberg about the Kennedy assassination? Is this important? Why am I remembering it? It must be important, that bullet smashing into the President's temple...? The murder of the mind by armed ideologues?

"Hank and Chuckie have written book after book about the primal field. It's all they care about. Thoughts rapidly appearing and disappearing, out of control and therefore of no use to the thinker—turn out to be just the opposite, perfectly controlled and supremely utile. These unstoppable eruptions are not disasters, but conscious life in an ideal state. The life of a thought is like the life of a breath. Breathing is thinking, thinking is breathing. Any interference is perceived just as a killer's hands feel around your throat. Breathe in the yin, breathe out the yang. Each thought becomes its opposite, which in turn becomes *its* opposite. All thoughts are natural. There is no coercion. When there is coercion, thoughts become unnatural. But this too is subject to change. Tyrants are killed by mobs and the mobs become tyrannical. This social phenomenon happens as well in the brain an infinite number of times every second. Go to the source. Thought is subatomic. Do not harness it. Express it."

"The source," says Nadia, "is God, and expressions of God are Love."

"What a pleasant thought, Nadia! Good luck with that!"

"Extolling the metaphysical, eschewing the actual! Some things never change!"

His father laughs, as this is pretty funny. George laughs into his pillow: *mff mff mff*. He doesn't really know who these people are, Mother, Father, the other identifiers and identities that allow them, or rather cause their positions to be locatable on the psychosocial navigation grid, to be used and abused by superficial people—but that doesn't mean he can't enjoy their witty company. The physical urge to laugh, with that laughter muffled by the pillow, leaps away from the pillow and becomes ungovernable, too loud, too long, he's panting in the dream with the terrible, exhausting force of it. For a moment, he listens in as Vladimir Nabokov discusses his novel, *Laughter in the Dark*.

His mother is sitting on the opposite side of a room, now clearly a bookstore, in Ithaca, New York, where George once worked. She is listening to Nabokov as well. *There's no way*, George thinks, *she's ever read a single word of his.* He resents her presence. His father has read Nabokov. Why isn't he here?

He realizes he can see nothing now. He looks and looks but comes up with nothing. *My eyes are wide open. Why can't I see?* Then he understands that he can see, and what he *is* seeing is nothing. The nothing that is, and the nothing that is not. *That's not Nabokov! Who said that?*

The blobs of watery chemicals stretched out on sticks who mean so much to other people—but strangely not to him, for whom they might as well be Martians—the "Mom" and the "Dad," have been arguing for hours and hours, without cease during the equally ceaseless night, and have reached an orchestral crescendo. A conductor with long white hair is making megalomaniacal gestures as he weaves the fabric of sound.

"Crazy people like me," says Nadia, "crazy people like me and *you*, Georgie-porgie—"

"I'm not crazy," he whispers, "just a little weird around the edges." His father chuckles amiably. The vortex sucks up both speech and laughter, spins them around in the manner of a toilet bowl, and makes them disappear. George remembers something about a septic tank, and someone hoping it would hold, out there in the twilight of the backyard, somewhere.

"*Crazy people like all three of us* and now let me finish.

We are very near the source, the field, the whatever you two men, you two big babies, want to call it, but we apprehend these fragments or whispers or molecules of creative energy as irreconcilable with common sense. They are intractable and impermanent but powerful and active: they are useless but cannot be ignored. So we mutter and shout our descriptions of these mercilessly emergent thoughts, the good thought, the evil thought, the smart, the stupid, the pleasant and the unpleasant, the memory of something and the imagination of its twin, and as we listen to ourselves we begin to see patterns. These patterns illustrate how a thought begins and how it ends: the field, the universal source, the original condition, which is—I'll be candid with you because I respect both of you— *God*. We who are close to God suffer the consequences of listening. We are driven mad by what we call hallucinations. Not the other way around! Madness does not produce hallucination. Hallucinations cause madness. But we offer up these hallucinations as genuine transmissions from God. We are crucified by these thoughts, just like the delusional wandering rabbi, Yeshua the Anointed, but offer them to our families and friends and neighbors and strangers as worthy of their attention, as valuable if translated properly. It's never translated properly though, is it. The Bible itself is just a latrine of willful mistranslations and bullshit commentary, but that's just because of the yin and yang of things. He said, she said, the telephone game, and so on. There never has been and never will be more than one story to tell. The Buddhists speak of the ten thousand things, and it's true that the variations of the stories of things, just as the number of fools, is infinite, *that* story featuring *this*, *this* story featuring *that*, and mine featuring me, yours featuring you, variations, we say, of a species that all seem plainly and simply different, but the truth is that the genus, the family, the order, the class phylum kingdom, the domain where the bacteria and archaea and eukaryotes find distinction—these are all one with the deuterium and protium and quantum fluctuations of the *Fragor Magnus*."

Holy Shit, thinks George. *She's quoting me.*

"Mom, you're quoting me."

"Of course I am! Who do you think I am?"

"Credit me or knock it off. I'm a copyleft person, so you're free to use my work, but you must credit it."

His father interrupts him. "This is all well and good, Nadia, but here we are in the real world and you're insisting dogs must tortured for people to be happy and succeed in life."

"I do not torture dogs."

"Oh yes you do."

"Dogs sometimes torture me, but never the other way around."

"This horrifying 'learned helplessness' that comes only from torture is central to the thinking at Penn's Positivity and Cheerfulness Institute—which you and your authoritarian husband 'make possible' with your gifts."

"Yes, and here we are in the real world where you can only find happiness and success by taking mescaline and *amanita muscaria*."

"That's absolutely true! I trip and you torture. I don't see much of a choice there. Anyhoo, Georgie boy, I met a group of French and American actors who are planning to spend half their time performing in Paris, and half in Minneapolis. I want to help them, and help them help us, so I am excited to hear you're involved with theater. Your uncle is on friendly terms with the Vice President of Finance at Medtronic, who has agreed to develop and sit on a board for the group. Through him and many others, I've found sponsors and backers who have power, money, status, and influence, international and national, and right there in Minnesota. The school will be built around a big old run-down house, one of the oldest in the county, that had once been the home of the mayor of Jackson, a man who had also been a Grand Dildo in the KKK, in the middle of whose term yours truly was born."

And then that poor demented soldier-boy killed you, Dad. And it all came to naught. It all comes to naught. Something always becomes nothing. Right, Mom? Right, Dad?

But his father and mother were no longer there.

23

In which the Creative Writers appear, tie George down as the Lilliputians did Gulliver, and threaten to torture the Negative Creativity out of him.

In their place, the Creative Writers appear. They have cleared some of the bodies of the film crew, and have tied George down, like the Lilliputians did Gulliver. They are crawling all over him with antlike determination, though he doesn't quite understand what's going on. All he can see of his surroundings is smoke and unearthly light. Then he gets it: it's a show trial! His potential success as a filmmaker has made him a target they cannot afford to leave alone and simply hope for the best. He is, they shout in thrilling unison, *an existential threat to creativity!*

"Everybody has had a bellyful of so-called civil liberties and fake freedoms of the Constitution," says Orgí, mopping her brow and grinning like Fredric March as William Jennings Bryan during the Scopes Monkey Trial. She is wearing a bald cap to accentuate the resemblance.

Alice has had a hundred surgeries and now looks like Lauren Bacall. "All those... *freedoms*. They haven't exactly... *worked out*, have they. I mean, the way everybody thought they would, hmmm?"

Billy Greggs and Harry Lorenzo sing a plainsong duet which lists George Joutsen's crimes against creativity. One student complained that he was dismissive of logic-based, combinatorial number-placement puzzles. She had wished to compile a hundred such puzzles and provide captions for each, detailing time and place of completion, and a five-star rating of how hard each had been.

"All I said was, I didn't know what Sudoku was."

"You're out of orrrrrder," sings Billy Bass.

"You're out of order!" shouts Al Pacino.

"Ignorance is no excuuuuuse," sings Harry Countertenor.

"Yes it is!"

"Your hostility to unconventional narratives is evidence of Dark Creativity!" shouts Orgí from the bench, still pretending to wipe sweat from her face as it's the only bit of stage biz she could come up with.

"You what?"

"More than one student," purrs Alice throatily, "complained that you did not talk slowly enough, or raise the pitch of your voice, or use simplified language structures."

"Aw come on now, Reznya, jeez."

"You consistently failed to exaggerate enunciation and repeat words they didn't know."

"Children around the world have thrilled to my exaggerated enunciation!"

"Lying to the court is a crime as well."

"Hy-per-bo-lee. Eye-ron-ee."

"Says here yer an anti-Semite, too," drawls Orgí.

"Oh shut up. I showed them a Nina Paley cartoon called 'This Land is Mine.'"

"Seems you got a little on the colorful side with one student. Says you called him an asshole in front of the whole class. Now surely that was dark creativity, wouldn't you agree, Professor Jetson?"

"He was watching a video on his phone while we were workshopping his insipid self-aggrandizement. He was so absorbed in it, I was able to walk up behind him and watch it myself."

"What then, sir, was the young fellow watching?"

"Road Karma. And he didn't respond when I called him an asshole. Somebody else must have told him about it afterwards."

"You mocked the very idea of trigger warnings. What say you to that, Herr Professor?"

"You *Schwein Hund*!"

"Come now, Professor, did you or did you not mock trigger-warnings."

"Well, yeah, because at first I thought it was a joke."

"It is no laughin' matter, suh!"

"What were we all supposed to do? Get up and leave? Let her read to an empty room? Wait for the terrifying sentence and then make a run for it? Clap our hands over our ears? Say *blah blah blah* real loud? How were we to know we'd be offended or whatever it is that happens in these things until we heard the essay? I figured it was just brand-promotion, right? *I'm going to get saucy or raw or uncompromising and unflinching in my examination of my feelings? You know, wait for it, it's going to be explosive and real, I call it like I see it?* I just didn't get it. And when she read the essay, I just looked around the room, waiting for someone to clue me in, but everybody seemed as bored as they usually were."

"Did it never, suh, I say did it nevuh occur to you that they were bored with your consistent rejection of the Rules for Creative Writers?"

"It did in fact occur to me. That's when I decided to up the ante and bring my *commedia dell'arte* skills into play."

"You refer, suh, to the uh, cream-pie, is that right?"

"I do indeed, suh!"

"So you admit you ah guilt-eh!"

"Sure. Whatever."

Alice says smokily that the court recognizes his

confession and repentant spirit, and therefore wishes to give him his old job back. Well, if not exactly his old job, something similar. He would have to formally renounce Dark Creativity, and promise not to make any more movies about war and murder and madness unless it was clear who was evil and who was good.

"No ambiguity, old man!" she sang out in a luxurious alto. "Ambiguity is imperialist, elitist, and smug, oh my! Lions and tigers and bears, oh my!"

"Well, you're being kinda ambiguous about what Dark Creativity is."

"Positive Creativity," purring and smiling sexily now, "is linked to beneficial outcomes. Those 9/11 terrorists are better understood and more correctly designated as Enemies of the Creative State."

"I couldn't agree with you more!"

"You can't agree with us?"

"CAN'T AGREE WITH YOU *MORE!*"

"How much more, hypothetically, in altered circumstances, *could* you agree with us?"

"I AGREE WITH YOU TOTALLY AND COMPLETELY!"

"Well, why didn't you say so in the first place, hmmm?"

George begins to struggle angrily with the ropes binding him.

"Our Mission is to stop Negative Creativity in its tracks, around the world and here at home. Terrorism, scams, fraud, ambiguity, irony, cynicism, failure to live strictly and happily in the here and now of the senses while extolling and excusing as natural and real the sorcery of the deepest and darkest corners of the psyche, blaspheming about the Sacred Free Speech when you know in your heart that free, benevolent, creative speech can only be truly performed in the service of those who have no voice, people whose voices need Amplification and Elevation™—I refer to one of our suites of programs. All forms of malevolence will eventually be stamped out, because only small bands of evil people wish to propagate negativity, but we must use our scientific knowledge of creativity to grind the flaming, oily buttocks of Hell's most brutish and ugly demons on all would-be malevolent creators. You see what you drove Student Super Z to do. Your friends and family are all dead. This is only just. Any punishment that does not end in death is no punishment at all. And of course the greatest crimes are punished eternally, in Hell, where no one is creative at all. If you wish to remain alive and creative, you must play by *our* rules. With Super Yin and change out of the way, our stability will be our greatest triumph. Now, all you have to do is swear on *The Creative Writer's Bible* and kiss the Flag of the Creative Writers: whadaya say, old pal?"

"I shit on the bible and use the flag to wipe myself."

George snaps the two-pound-test monofilament restraining his wild fury. He rises up bellowing, shits a ton of doubloons, and stomps on his colleagues. They explode like tomatoes and whisper their hatred in pools of juice. This is really all he ever wanted to do.

24

In which a stable reality holds Ann and George in its embrace as they circle the Earth in their satellite home and watch the rushes of A Heap of Gold. Super Yin and Fred commune in silent darkness.

In a small screening room, the last scene of George and Ann's movie is being shown: Ann shrieking, wings on fire, George's cartoon face struck with unimaginable horror, explosion, fade to black.

They can't see each other, and content themselves with the sound of sighs, sounds of drinking, shifting in their seats. Slowly they begin to make each other out, dark shapes against a brilliantly starry sky. Then they see glints of the glass bubble in which they are floating. George drifts to another part of the bubble and stares at the big blue planet.

"Still there," he says.

"We don't have an ending," sighed Ann.

"Don't we?"

"We do not."

"The explosion will have to do."

"Well. It's not like it'll be the first movie to end by blowing shit up."

"Sigh," says George. "Nothing is real, not even the movie."

"Especially the movie."

A space-car pulls into the bubble's lower port. Judy and Henrik and too many children to count spill out of it, wearing jetpacks and helmets. They buzz about and play and sing.

"Dad," says Judy, "the kids were playing with the monitors of the oldest stars, and were laughing so much I had to find out what was so funny."

"What was so funny?"

"Well, it's not."

"What is it then?"

"The old stars seem to be...going out."

The night sky does seem somewhat less brilliant, George thinks, than it had only a moment earlier. Ann drops toward them, throwing out her wings for a delicate landing that is increasingly difficult for her.

"I just checked the thermometer," she says. "The sun is cooler. Not much, but still...."

Twilight is deepening on Lake Superior. Trees have lost their leaves and the wind off the lake is very strong. The water is purple with whitecaps. Fred, hobbled and old, wearing his old orange and black rags and using a cane, has arrived after a long walk on the narrow road to the deep north. A dog accompanies him. He sits on a rock and takes paper and pen from his sack.

He reads aloud what he writes:

"Blessed twilight comes.

The purple and green water.

Narrow road, deep north."

He ceases to speak and worships the Silence. After some time he hears the buffeting of his cloak by the wind and the slow, heavy movement of water on rocks.

"After many days of solitary wandering, I have come to the great gate of the north. The actors are dead and their acts forgotten."

He listens for the sonic booms that only he can hear, but there are none. There have been none for a very long time.

He continues his worship of the Silence for a long time, broken only by the sound of waves and wind. Then he hears a distinct pop, as if someone had stuck a finger in his mouth and popped his cheek.

Super Yin trudges toward him, finger to her old lips.

The sun goes out and the Earth is as if it had never been.

A moment later, light begins to seep out of the nothing and into the something.

THE END

OR IS IT?

ACKNOWLEDGEMENTS

I thank at the molecular level five literary bodhisattvas, without whom the last decade would have been an unrelieved hell of unpublishable novels becoming unwritable novels: Tom Smuts, John Richardson, Rick Harsch, Lee Thompson, and Bill Clarke.

Gary Amdahl is the author of *Visigoth* (2006), *I Am Death* (2008), *The Intimidator Still Lives in Our Hearts* (2013), *Across My Big Brass Bed* (2014, 2023), *The Daredevils* (2016), and *Much Ado About Everything: Oration on the Dignity of the Novelist* (2016).

Printed in the USA
CPSIA information can be obtained
at www.ICGtesting.com
JSHW021628071024
70788JS00005B/121